GW00857311

THE ARTIST'S RIVAL

EMILY HAYES

1

TATIANA

To accompany the sky's rumbling thunder, Tatiana Khan's brushes fall to the floor. She bends to pick them up, weary from work. The still moist leftovers of paint on their hair splash all over the wood, creating vivid bursts of color.

"Ah, Pollock," she sighs.

Grabbing a wet rag to clean up the mess, she shakes her head at the overused joke. The yellow paint stains her fingers, slimy and yolk-like. Wanting to get up, she reaches for the table's support, inattentively leaving yellow marks behind. *A sign to finish work*, she nods. *I am leaving behind trails of sun*, she recites, trying to remember the poem without success.

Making her way to the bathroom, Tatiana has to jump over her crumbled messes, belongings laying in strange combinations. Tangles of clothes stretch and curl, intertwined so tightly and chaotically that one could mistake them for lovers, sprawled around the wooden panels. The fabrics seem almost to breathe, in and out, flowing with the animal rhythm of deep sleep. She likes the image and reaches for her sketchbook instead of the bathroom door.

She draws a stormy riverside, maybe abandoned. Women, wanting to wash their clothes, could be driven away by the harsh weather; they have left in haste. Out of their baskets dark shirts and undergarments must have fallen, tossed about by the wind. The tumbling materials stretch out on the sand, wild, unintelligible. Their outlines speak to an animal quality—when she draws them captured in motion, their sleeve limbs appear to run. Here and there, the sketch is marked by traces of warm yellow paint, still stuck to her fingers. Satisfied with the idea, she leaves the sketchbook on the floor, determined to finally wash her hands and rest.

The switch clicks and a flood of bathroom light hits her eyes with a piercing harshness, putting in spotlight the toothpaste-stained sink. Solitude seems to double Tatiana's tendency to forego cleaning. It also seems to triple her artistic potency, which is how she has been justifying leaving sinks cluttered, floors littered, and bedsheets unchanged. She can easily disregard caring for her space when she thinks of it more as a studio, rather than home. Sometimes she wonders whether her unwillingness to rent a space to paint truly comes from financial motivations as opposed to her liking this state of intimacy with art, unseparated from her private life and over-flowing in every room.

–

"Come on, Terry's playing tonight!" Connie shouts on the phone.

It's pouring heavily, and Tatiana looks out the window in resignation. She shivers, thinking of stepping outside into the mud, bathing in evening rainwater.

"The weather's horrible," she says, all the same slowly letting go of her plans for a peaceful night inside.

"Good thing the club has a roof," Connie

concludes, hanging up with a brief, "See you there!"

With no heart to dim her friend's excitement, Tatyana begins dressing up to go. Stumbling over piles of belongings, she manages to dig out some clothes of dubious cleanliness. To remedy the uncertainty, she buries her face right in, smelling only the reassuringly delicate scent of the laundry detergent. Notes of vanilla stroke her skin as she shuts her eyes close, preparing to face the unpleasant air outside.

Tatiana, now ironing her shirt, craves to feel the hot steam with each lifting of the iron, trying to get all the warmth it can afford her. She doesn't tolerate cold weather well. Each year, unable to contain her excitement for spring, she ends up spending too much on summertime clothes, later lost in the pits of her wardrobe. Linen dresses and light cotton underwear wink at her seductively from every spring clothing collection.

In childhood, this aversion towards winter often sparked good-natured teasing from her parents, entertained to see their daughter grow up far from the freezing land of her grandfathers. A child who doesn't know the true winter, they'd laugh.

Driving to the venue, she yawns, but is glad to be going out. Ever since parting ways after art school, she and Connie rarely spend time together, torn between careers and bigger or smaller loves. Without Connie and other friends, Tatiana would probably lose her sanity. Working on her art for hours in solitude makes her mind tender to sound and light. To create, she must exaggerate each state of feeling, letting it flow onto the canvas. Whenever a wave of inspiration hits, she refuses to pause, afraid of affecting the quality of her creation. Afterwards, even though satisfied, she often finds herself weary of her own thoughts, sensitive and estranged from conversation. *An animal in a cave,* she muses. Friends are often an artist's saviors.

The radio remains turned off, letting the gentle sound of rain fill her car with its simmering, static noise. Little droplets hit the windshield bringing back images of hours spent driving around in the backseat of her father's car, filling her mind to the brim with a familiar, nostalgic fog. Racing rain drops, swimming down like thin veins, inspired a ton of her early drawings. She stops, seeing the vibrant light of the club's entrance dance around through the streaks of water. The strokes of light dissolve in her relaxed eyes, colors blend into each other. She sits still for a moment, taking in the impressionist beauty of the scene.

—

"Terry, congratulations!" She embraces the young man, taking a seat by the bar with Connie, watching him get on stage.

Terry is a perplexing character, entirely unsure of what path he wants to commit to. The only consistent thread in his life, as far as Tatiana can tell, is his love affair with music. As long as he's on stage, he seems to be doing fine.

"So... He no longer plays the piano?" She leans in to whisper to Connie's ear.

"No, No. He prefers wind instruments now. Tonight, it's the trumpet."

"How does he even do that?"

Connie chuckles, light-hearted. She has a delightful chuckle, sweet and chiming like small, high-pitched bells.

"It's the curse of being young, Tat," she

explains. "They're good at everything and can't choose anything."

"Maybe you're right," Tatiana responds, turning to order a drink.

Deep down, however, she's pondering her friend's words. Terry's constant indecision seems foreign to her. As a child she knew what drew her in, and in a self-perpetuating cycle of practice and praise, she was certain she had found her true calling. Granted, she always felt blessed to be graced by the guidance from her parents, sure to be by her side as she kept working on her craft. Of course, she gave other visual arts a try, but always circled back to pencils and brushes, finding that these infrequent departures only deepened her relationship with painting. In photography, she found self-expression to be too limited for her taste, nonetheless learning from it the importance of light. Light entered her paintings like a phantom, setting the ambience of the entire scenery. Not many people pay attention to light while admiring a painting, even though that is its main component. Her father made sure to teach Tatiana sculpture; his eyes tearing up as he watched her chisel the way into the stone. Working with such an unforgiving material taught her invaluable lessons, infusing her own art with a persistent appreciation for form. From each art she could borrow from, she did, but always faithfully making her way back to the love of her life, painting.

At the opposite end, there was Terry—a tangle of aspirations and talent out of which something resembling a troubled artistic soul emerged, playing for pennies at bars and picking up girls after each show. For now, Connie was the girl for him, just as the trumpet was the instrument. Whatever he'd play next will probably replace the trumpet, just as soon as his infatuation with Connie will come to pass, replaced by another girl, Tatiana is sure. *At least for him the pool seems infinite*, she concludes, slightly bitter. In the artistic community, queer women seem to be caught in their own webs the moment they step in, and everyone is somehow tied to one another, entangled in sticky webs of longing and memories. Back in college, Connie and Tatiana used to have late night conversations spinning until morning hours, comparing their lives.

The band starts playing, and the chatter quiets down, making the few surviving conversations more sharply defined. The strings of singular voices tingle Tatiana's ears, making it impossible not to casually eavesdrop. She's not feeling very passionate about jazz music.

"Ah yes, I've been to the gallery." A clumsy whisper makes its way to Tatiana across the bar.

A young pair, apparently finding it impossible to keep quiet, exchange some recent experiences with the art scene of the city, hunched over their drinks.

The woman, girl, really, resembles Tatiana's old friends from college—her clothes and hairstyle communicating an avid interest in art, or perhaps fashion. Her dangling pearl earrings reflect beautifully the dim light above the bar. The sparkle carries a tinge of warmth.

"What'd you think about the new painter there?" asks the boy, in no whisper at all.

If Tatiana cared about the musical performance, their conversation would be annoying.

"The woman?" The girl continues without hearing the answer, "I thought her paintings seemed very...serene? Very calming."

"Definitely. I liked them a lot." The boy shifts on his seat, finishing his martini. "Some of the best landscapes out there right now, for sure," he states, self-assured.

Tatiana, now particularly invested in the conversation, decides to join in and inquire about the artist, unsure whether she recognizes the gallery. Carefully picking up her purse, she leaves the transfixed Connie in favor of the loud couple, ready to investigate.

"Excuse me," she smiles. "I overheard you talk about painting, and wanted to ask—"

She sits down next to them, already a bit sorry to interrupt. But the pair seems welcoming.

"Do you remember the name of the artist?" A tinge of hope decorates the last syllables of her question, hung in the air vibrating with jazz. Not many people remember contemporary artists' names, but the boy visibly wants to impress his companion, straining his memory.

"Umm..." He furrows his brows, focused, "some generic surname, like... Matthews? Yeah, Matthews, I think. I don't know the first name," he says, beaming with pride.

"Alright, thanks a lot anyway. Are you two art students?" Tatiana asks, always invested in seeking out budding artists.

"I am." The girl smiles, leaning in closer not to shout over the music, though the piece is just coming to an end. "I study sculpture at the university nearby."

"Sculpture! That's beautiful!" Tatiana's eyes shine. "Are you familiar with Dominik Khan, by any chance?"

"Yes, I've been to see a live interview with him recently." The crowd erupts with applause for the music.

"You know, he's my father," Tatiana states, proudly.

The pair turn out to be very perceptive and knowledgeable, making the evening particularly pleasant for Tatiana. Their conversation flows, weaving in its fabric various subjects dear to her heart, such as artistic legacy and subverting tradition. Talking with young artists and art enthusiasts never fails to amaze Tatiana. She grows excited to see what the future brings for art, recognizing in the students the same sensitivity that drew her towards creating. She buys the pair a drink each and makes her way back to her original seat.

Something weighs heavy on her, however. Remembering their initial conversation, she feels unprofessional, not having heard of the rising talent already getting exhibited. Even though landscapes are her domain, she has no idea about this person. She takes out her phone, and blinded by the screen's light, notes down *Matthews - paintings.* Curiosity bubbles in her chest.

Connie seems to be having a good time, talking to Terry and his band. She looks charming in her teal dress, as if fresh out of an art deco painting. Tatiana always thought her much too good for all the men she chose to date.

"Where did you disappear?" Connie turned to welcome Tatiana into the conversation. Her cheeks seemed slightly blushed with wine.

"I learned something interesting," Tatiana raises her voice over the room's chatter. "A painter I haven't heard of is exhibiting her landscapes."

Terry laughs.

"I don't get why you choose to paint these boring things," he shakes his head, dismissively.

"Terry, stop being an asshole," interrupts Connie. "Landscapes can convey a lot of emotion. And especially if you understand the traditions, you can see how a painter chooses to interpret them."

"That's some art school talk." He turns to order another drink.

"And what have you been working on, recently?" Tatiana asks Connie, wishing to move past the unpleasant exchange.

"A new collage for some gallery." Connie shrugs. "I'm not happy with it at all, but I need commissions, so..."

Tatiana nods, feeling the weariness of the day on her shoulders. She considers buying another drink, as she would usually do, but decides against it. Besides, Terry is a real nuisance to be around, and she doubts she would get any meaningful conversation out of Connie in his vicinity.

"Listen, Con," she taps her friend's shoulder gently. "I think I'll head home, I'm very tired today."

Connie seems disappointed, but nods.

"Alright, get some rest. I'll talk to you soon, alright?" She turns to go along with the band. "And send me over the new artist, I'll check them out!" And having said so, she disappears into the crowd.

Tatiana's way to the exit is marked by constant bumping into cologne-smelling men or the purses of their companions. Once out, the rain hits her brutally. She keeps turning around to look for her car, lost amidst a never-ending sea of others. The unremarkable, silver thing goes unnoticed so easily that it gets on Tatiana's nerves with a

concerning regularity. Each evening out is a hopeless digging through piles of vehicles. She clicks
her keys in hopes of hearing the car's call.

Having finally found it, she feels a wave of grat-
itude so strong it warms up her whole body, impatient for a shower and some hot soup. Getting
inside, her soaking-wet clothes flood the seat,
making it cold and disgusting. The weather surely
soured the evening, she thinks, driving too fast for
the slippery roads, splashing some passersby on
accident. They wave at her angrily as she speeds
away towards home.

—

As the leftover borscht is warming up in a
trusty, metal pot, Tatiana decides to search for
information on the mysterious landscape painter.
Matthews landscape painting.

The search turns out to be much quicker than
she expected. Multiple galleries advertise one Ellie
Matthews, shouting out critics' praise and show-
casing the rich tapestry of her portfolio. Looking
through the paintings, Tatiana can see how close
the subject matter stands to her own work. The
landscapes Matthews paints give voice to simple

objects enveloped by natural scenery. Little signs of humanity lay scattered amidst lakes and forests, filling the viewer's chest with something airy, like nostalgia. Childhood memories play around her somber trees, abandoned swings sit still, pensively. In other paintings, the sun bends low to kiss the earthy fields goodnight. The peaceful dance of Sun and Earth seems to go on indefinitely in her paintings, sometimes interrupted by the Moon. The sun seems to be made into a character on its own, tinting the sky into various moods. Matthews certainly values the delicate power of natural light, infusing her paintings with the harmonious power of nature valued so greatly in traditional landscape painting.

Something stirs within Tatiana, as she turns the phone off and walks towards the kitchen counter. The thick steam rising from the soup pot kisses her face. She pours herself a generous bowl and heads to her bed, feeling wrinkled and crumbled like a tormented napkin. Matthews' landscapes take place in similar states of mind, but her painting uses only very traditional tools. There is no bending of the form, which Tatiana adores so greatly. In her opinion, the paintings are technically good, but don't seem to ask any thought-provoking questions. In Tatiana's eyes, they prioritize the aesthetic homage to the artists of the past, which makes her question their value today.

They lack my courage, Tatiana tells herself. *They're an ode to romanticism, not an original notion.* She nods, eating spoonfuls of borscht, listening to the storm outside.

Who is this Ellie Matthews, anyway?

2

ELLIE

Ellie Matthews is harshly stirred out of her blissful sleep, woken up by the noise of her alarm clock. Cozy and buried in her bedsheets, she watches as the clock vibrates on its shelf, heading inevitably towards its own undoing. She has no strength to leave the bed, softly ensconced in her baby blue sheets, warm and untouchable, allowing the small disaster to unfold.

The alarm clock falls to the floor with a crash, putting an end to its annoying ring.

Pathetic, it lays on its face. Touched by pity towards the little thing, Ellie finally drags herself out of the bed. The cold, laminated floor stings her feet, and the room's air seems very unwelcoming.

She picks up the cheap clock, the glass cracked from its fall. Now a sense of guilt climbs up her stomach. She decides to treat it as hunger and remedy it by having a fresh breakfast.

Ever since moving to the city, Ellie has been utterly in love with the neighborhood's bustling morning market, held every Saturday and Sunday in an old hangar only a few streets away from her apartment. Picking out her dress, she can already smell the mountains of produce colorfully stacked inside the old hangar, spices and teas swirling in the air, and fresh-caught fish slid into shopping bags. Keys in her hand, she's on the way.

–

Strolling around the alleys, Ellie finds herself discreetly people-watching. It always happens to her unintentionally, the short glances gradually lingering longer, turning sticky. Her eyes stick to people from afar, families shopping for the day and relaxing to the beat of a Saturday morning; daughters push little wired shopping carts, sons run around their mothers' legs, couples embrace each other tenderly.

The tendency to linger and observe has always

been present in Ellie's life. Even as a child, she would often look from a distance—watch, as life displayed its beauty in front of her. No wonder she has always felt drawn to conveying what she saw. Through painting, she could show the beauty back to the world.

An appealing stand with bright red strawberries calls out to her impatiently. As she bends low to smell them, their sweet scent fills her nostrils with a promise of an even sweeter taste. Looking for her wallet, she decides on a fruit breakfast. Baskets of berries and oranges seem irresistible, a small invitation for spring to finally unleash itself. Packing everything into her wicker basket, she whistles a joyful tune.

—

Unpacking the fragrant fruits on her counter, she sets a pot of oatmeal to cook. Ellie commits to preparing her meals with undivided attention, savoring the moment of cooking with joy. In her view, artists especially have the responsibility of experiencing the world richly and attentively, developing a much-needed sensitivity of all the senses. She watches as the steam rises from the pot while cutting apples and peeling oranges. Her cupboard is sure to always be filled with various high-quality spices; a practice she owes to her father. His absolute mastery of the kitchen filled her childhood with joyful hours of cooking together, preparing meals with love and attention. He made sure his daughters would appreciate the flavorful cuisine of his grandfathers, carrying on the numerous recipes and traditions.

Reminiscing, she adds spices to the pot. Nutmeg, cinnamon, ginger, and honey make her oatmeal divine.

Sitting down to eat, she receives an avalanche of messages from her friend, Frank, apparently very excited: *Have you seen her yet??*

Ellie opens the attachments, quickly learning of an artist making waves in the city, a modern landscape painter, Tatiana Khan. The surname rings some bells, but Ellie is unsure whether it's not a coincidence; she doesn't seem to be familiar with the work. That marks a surprising discovery, seeing the subject matter is so close to her own paintings—or at least, the subject matter used to subvert what Ellie paints.

Khan's paintings occupy the territory of experimental landscapes, the compositions often unexpectedly erupting with vibrant color unfounded within the context of the space. Looking through the painter's body of work, Ellie finds a painting particularly similar to one of her own, portraying a little hilltop with a swing, hung from a widely branching tree. She admires the skill of Khan's background hills, enveloped still by the morning mist. The sun is on its way to rise, timidly gleaming from amidst the still-dark trees. The swing seems recently abandoned, in the middle of its course. To portray its motion, Khan decided to abandon the painting's classical form and dash thick white paint atop it, marking the swing's trajectory. This work angers Ellie, who can already imagine the shallow praise it probably received. Critics would gasp over the meaningful boldness of subverting such a beautiful form.

Ellie keeps looking, other paintings employ different tools but with the same bold disregard. She realizes the emotions conveyed through Khan's art relate deeply to the sentiments of her own work, often portraying abandoned spaces or landscapes including minuscule traces of humanity. Only Ellie's work employs subtlety and doesn't look to disregard the form where it is unnecessary.

Looking to find Khan's age, her suspicions stand confirmed; Tatiana is ten years her junior.

How do you like it? She asks Frank. He is a painter of his own renown, and his reflections on art never fail to remain on point.

A creeping distaste haunts Ellie. She doesn't understand why Khan's paintings would garner such recognition when, clearly, they're only meant to be aggressively postmodern.

I think she manages the concept well, the paintings are touching. It's not my style, but she's clearly very skilled.

Frank's response doesn't settle any of Ellie's feelings. Having finished the bowl of oatmeal, she busies herself with doing the dishes until the phone's ringing interrupts her.

"Did you forget about our call?" the familiar, sunny voice flows through the speaker.

"Hi Mom, I completely forgot today's Saturday," Ellie explains, happy to hear her mother.

"How are you doing, dear? Everything going well with the exhibition?"

"Yes, I'm opening a new one soon," her voice beams with pride. "I have a question—"

Ellie stirs a bit. Her mother's opinions on art still carry a lot of importance for her.

"Do you recognize this new painter, Tatiana Khan?" Ellie pauses. "She seems to be gaining a lot of recognition here recently, and she also does landscapes."

"Tatiana Khan... No, not really. But you know, I'm not as up to date as I used to be, these days." She pauses to think some more. "Is she related to Dominik Khan, by any chance?"

"I don't know. Who's that?"

"Oh, a very successful sculptor of my generation. Our paths never crossed, but I heard a great deal about him."

And so their weekly conversation would run its course, little waves of insignificant details from their daily lives, opinions on recently read books, art exhibitions, news about friends.

"I'm thinking of creating something new, I have these images following me around recently. I think it could be beautiful," admits Ellie.

"Don't tell me anything!" laughs her mother. "It brings bad luck to talk about unmade art. Go and paint," she advises. "Go and paint it."

"Well, now I just might." Ellie shakes her head to herself, always entertained by her mom's superstitions. "Say hi to Dad for me, will you?"

"Sure. He'll be visiting soon."

After hanging up, a sense of familiar gloom overcomes Ellie. The warmth of her mother's voice seemed more tinted with pain than the last time they talked, words took on different shapes in her mouth than usual. The conversations keep getting harder for her, a pulsing reminder of her absence from her family's life and struggles. Though the doctors keep reassuring the family of high chances for recovery, Ellie still feels discomfort being so far away from them during the difficult time. The only way for her to justify not taking care of her mother in person is to make her art career worth every minute away from her hometown.

With thoughts of recent successes swimming around her mind, Ellie takes her mother's advice and decides to get working on her recent vision.

Driving to the newly rented studio, she focuses on the images she has been stumbling into. Images of cascading water, bathed by the dusking sun. She wonders whether it somehow corresponds to the fear for her mother, subconsciously gushing out into her art. She shakes her head to drive the thought away.

Ellie's mother holds a strong conviction that one should never analyze one's own art, only leave it to the audience and the critics. Whenever Ellie would begin guessing what the elements of her paintings could mean, her mother would interrupt, believing that creation and analysis do not belong to the same process. The artist's task is to create raw and honest art. The water would cascade.

Ellie parks and gets out the keys to her studio. She still is barely able to believe the success her art has recently achieved, affording her a spacious apartment together with a spacious studio, something she has been dreaming about since leaving art school. The key shines in her hand, as she climbs the stairs.

Once the door stands open, she inhales the strong smell of acrylic paint and feels at home. The bright space embraces her with light, and she gets her materials ready to sketch. While working, she notices that the mood of the painting will vary drastically from her usual, more melancholy, state. The waterfall seems to require grandeur, and together with the dying sun, the painting seems to rage. She sees the water below rippling, struck by the continuous flow from above, heavy and unforgiving. Hills stand bare, birthing this falling water, shining with the red reflections of dusk. The sketch has no color, but she can see exactly where the red should lick the painting.

Taking a break, she stands up to look at the sketch from afar. The style of the piece resembles more the work she used to create a few years ago, making her question the inspiration, despite her mother's words. Her stomach rumbles, and she decides to take a break for lunch.

Hey Fred, are you in the city? She texts, changing from her work clothes back to her dress. Fred owns a studio a few streets away, so they often eat out together.

Getting a sandwich, wanna join?

Walking to the sandwich shop, Ellie can't let go of the surprising nature of her new project. Fred is known to shift his style aggressively and often, and she knows that he will be quick to belittle her confusion. The friends hug upon seeing each other.

"Ellie! How's it going?" Fred exclaims in between enormous bites of his salmon sandwich.

"I began working on something," Ellie begins, going over the menu trying to decide between vegetables and tuna, "and the project really surprises me."

Having chosen the eggplant grand sandwich, she sits down to join Fred at the table.

"Tell me more," he says.

"You know my recent pieces, I thought I finally found my style and a consistent voice," she explains, "but this... It's been haunting me for weeks, and once I finally begin sketching, it seems completely different from all my recent work. Very... aggressive."

Fred nods. He swallows the last bits of his lunch, and chooses his response carefully, knowing Ellie's approach to be very different from his own.

"Why don't you just flow with the piece, see where it takes you? You don't really need to sell anything at the moment, so feel free to experiment."

Ellie looks away.

"I think I'm trying to prove something," she admits. "With this new rival landscape artist."

Fred laughs, amused.

"Tatiana Khan? Oh please, there is enough room for the two of you. I got to know her recently, she's charming."

Tatiana is charming? huh.

Ellie doesn't want to talk about Tatiana Khan,

but the thought of her remains stuck in Ellie's mind. She feels silly, being influenced by insecurity or some strange competitiveness. She knows Fred is right, and there is more than enough space in the city for two landscape painters but feeling that Khan's art represents something she disagrees with, Ellie feels the need to prove her own style's right to be. They talk of the upcoming exhibitions and their shared friend's new book, before Tatiana Bloody Khan is brought up again.

"By the way," says Fred, slowly gathering his things up to go. "I'm hosting a dinner party next weekend, and Tatiana is going to be there. Would you like to come?"

"Well... Sure," she says, before giving it much thought.

Ellie rarely rejects invitations.

Having parted with Fred, however, she begins to really imagine how the party could go. Insecurity often gets the better of her, even though usually she's a sweet and encouraging person, especially with respect to fellow artists. Making her way back up to the studio, she decides to remain hopeful. Perhaps the encounter will somewhat tame her ill thoughts about Khan's art, and they will emerge out of it as friends.

Returning to her sketch, she resolves to wait and see where the art takes her.

What will this Tatiana Khan be like?

3

TATIANA

"I'm five minutes away, Fred, I swear," Tatiana shouts into her malfunctioning car speaker and hangs up, annoyed at herself.

Per usual, she's failing to be on time—something she has sworn to work on again and again, endlessly having to apologize for her delays. Stuck in a traffic jam, she can feel her thoughts buzz with excitement and a tinge of anxiety. Having the chance to finally meet her rival, Ellie Matthews fills her chest with tingling, not knowing what to expect, really. The cars around her keep honking chaotically, aggravated men in expensive suits, in their expensive cars, try to outsmart everyone, unwittingly blocking the road even more. Clogged up in the middle of the lengthy string of cars shining in the afternoon sun, Tatiana can do nothing but open the window and wait, hoping that the wine bottle on her backseat will not warm up too much. She picked out the wine hastily hoping it would be a decent one, now worrying that she bought something distasteful. The air flowing into the tight space of her car finally smells of spring, sun-filled and fresh, calming her irritated nerves. The cars finally begin to move.

—

The doorbell seems stuck, worn out by time. Tatiana presses it repeatedly to no avail, resorting to banging on the sturdy door with her fist. Waiting for an answer to her knocking, she looks up.

What unravels above her can only be described as angelic. Tall trees in early bloom spread their light-pink branches in elaborate ways, delicate petals fall here and there, stroking the ground with blessings of this effortless beauty. Tatiana takes out her phone, in an attempt to capture the view. Unfortunately, the quality of her pictures turns out to be disappointing and inadequate. The flat, banal photos fail to translate her awe. *That's why painting exists,* she thinks to herself when the door finally swings open revealing Fred, elegantly dressed up.

"Oh, hello," he says, his face pretend-upset at her being late.

They embrace, feeling their budding friendship spark brighter with each meeting. Their interactions flow effortlessly, and friendly physical contact grows more frequent between them, in the light way friends have with each other.

Stepping in, Tatiana is led into a wide, sunny hall. The tall walls seem to breathe light; their warm, off-white color embraces its guest with a kind welcome. The decor is simple but tasteful, certainly adequate for an artist's dwelling. Spread around the floor, glass vases hold tall, vibrant flowers in them. Tatiana nods, approvingly.

"Quite a nice place you got there, Fred," she laughs.

"Feel free to take off your shoes or keep them on, whatever suits you," Fred offers, moving swiftly to another room, presumably the kitchen. Tatiana can already smell rich spices permeating the air as she hears light, giggly voices filling the dining space. She takes these little joys in, relieving herself of the anxieties for the moment.

She sets the wine bottle she brought on the hallway table and decides to keep her shoes on, thinking that her clothes look more complete this way. Taking off shoes always seemed very intimate to her, perhaps because in her family there was no strong custom surrounding going barefoot inside. Having taken off her coat, she makes her way to the dining room, once more welcomed by strong light, bathing the entire house. Large, door-sized windows stand shadowed only by delicate cyan curtains, and when her eyes begin to settle into this pool of brightness, she notices Ellie Matthews glancing curiously in her direction, sitting amidst the other—more or less known to Tatiana —guests.

When their eyes meet at first, the women scatter their gaze, not knowing how to handle the weight of expectations each harbors for the other. Their brief game of glances is jumpy, with rules unknown to either of them. Tatiana's eyes juggle between meeting Ellie's and sliding away towards the safety of the wall, the elaborate table decor, and some other guests. With mercy, Ellie at last rises from her seat, making her way around the table towards Tatiana, putting an end to their awkward dance. Her green eyes seem to sparkle with dim curiosity, veiled, perhaps, by manners, as she extends her hand, decorated by various jiggling bracelets and elaborate, golden rings that match her golden hair.

"Hello, you must be Tatiana Khan. Pleasure to meet you," she smiles.

Her voice has a particularly pleasant lilt Tatiana wasn't expecting to hear. Each syllable sounds honeyed and rich, as if smoothly caressed by her tongue. It's deep and golden, like a jar of honey left at a tabletop.

"Well, pleasure to finally meet you too, Ellie," Tatiana responds, shaking Ellie's hand. Not knowing what more she could say, Tatiana nods and makes her way towards the table.

Meanwhile, Fred emerges from the kitchen, carrying dishes of potatoes, carrots, and duck, delicious steam reaching everyone's noses and salivating their mouths.

"Thomas, could you help me, darling?" he cries out, almost tripping on the table's leg. Fortunately, none of the dishes fall, and he manages to set them all down.

Thomas quickly gets up, soon to disappear into

the kitchen. When he reemerges, everyone is asked to sit down and begin sharing the food. Chatter and clinking of cutlery fills the dining room, wine is poured into glasses, and Tatiana finds herself sitting opposite Ellie, trying to listen in to the conversation playing out between her and a talented young artist, Marceline.

The voices of the two women now and then smooth into polite laughter, and whenever that happens, Ellie's slightly glittering dress sparkles. Its black material has a glistening quality, enchanting to look at. Between the lively sparkle of her dress and the chiming of her jewelry, she looks quite remarkable to Tatiana.

"So... you don't like my pictures?" Marceline inquires jokingly, though behind the veil of laughter Tatiana can sense a shadow of offense.

"That's not at all what I'm trying to say," Ellie takes a sip of wine, straightening up. "I only think that sometimes, in search of more experimental methods, we lose our artistic sensitivity. Don't you agree?"

Something hot swirls around Tatiana's head when she hears Ellie's opinion, said a bit louder than the other parts of the conversation. She stabs a potato with her fork, confident in her suspicion that the remark was directed at her art, not Marceline's.

Is that right? Who made you the expert, Ellie fucking Matthews? Thinking herself to be too self-absorbed, however, she puts some more garlic potatoes on her plate and listens on, curious to see where the conversation will take them.

"What do you mean, exactly?" Marceline smiles, cutting the duck.

"Through adhering to the art form's conventions, though forever changing," Ellie makes sure to note, "an artist, in my opinion, can convey particularly subtle nuances in meaning. Well perceptible, while also, more often than not, aesthetically pleasing."

Her tone of voice did not contain even a note of condescension, though Tatiana could feel a sense of superiority in Ellie's choice of words. Hers, Tatiana begins to see now, is the approach to art often found within the elites, championing the notion of keeping up the sophistication and literacy of the art world. Literacy dictated by themselves, of course. Feeling strongly about the subject matter, she waits on the edge of her seat for a chance to speak up. She can see Marceline blush, visibly offended.

"Do you think that because my pictures mix forms and involve experimental elements, I lose the nuances of traditional photography?" She tries to match Ellie's casual tone but fails.

Tatiana barely knows Marceline, but even so, she is aware of the girl's hot-headedness. Even though only twenty-two, Marceline is already commonly thought of as a prodigy in terms of experimental photography, creating beautiful works combining picture-taking and painting. Tatiana is a great admirer of her work.

"Not at all, Marceline, I'm so sorry—" Ellie stumbles, put in an awkward position. "I only like to think about the shock value a lot of contemporary art employs, regarding the subject matter *or* the form itself," she digs her own grave further.

Tatiana catches Fred's nervous glance in her direction, and suddenly understands why he chose to invite the two of them to the dinner. While a wonderful artist and friend, she knows Fred to be quite conflict-seeking, entertained by drama and disagreements.

"Ellie," Tatiana finally decides to join in, "where would you draw the line, then? Between participating in the evolution of art and defying it by unnecessary transgression?"

Their eyes meet, Ellie's are a bright emerald green and she smiles showing off lovely neat white teeth. Tatiana can see that she's not used to conflict, the corners of her mouth curl slightly in discomfort.

Ugh, I hate her. And why does she have to be so frustratingly beautiful?

"That's definitely up for interpretation, but I would say that if an artist resorts to incorporating elements shockingly outside of the form, or seemingly in defiance of it—" here she stops for a moment, thinking, "which I'm unsure now how to define precisely, probably as a form of denial of some sort... Then they are relying on the transgressive nature of the artwork, not on its quality, or skill involved, or even the pure message."

Tatiana turns the argument over and over in her thoughts, nauseatingly familiar with the train of thought, but looking for the most compelling way to show how harmful such beliefs can be to the developing artists.

"Every style seemed pretty transgressive at the time of its birth," she says, carefully.

"For sure," agrees Ellie, clearly wanting to sneakily escape the conversation.

Soon, the subject fades away in favor of

others, and Tatiana turns to Thomas, having barely talked with him until now. They engage in casual small talk, and not having much in common with each other besides Fred, they naturally turn to the subject of his art. Fred's recent series of paintings exploring the theme of tears caused much stir in their circle. He built an entire installation made up of enormous glass drops made of crystal, reflecting light beautifully in little specks along the walls of his studio, only to then paint them, and dismantle the installation afterwards.

"Each time I go to see it, I find some new remarkable detail," Tatiana admits.

Thomas nods, proud of his fiancé.

"Are you guys not moving in together?" she asks, out of curiosity and lack of a better question.

"No, not yet," Thomas sighs, "we both really appreciate private space."

Fred interrupts, breaking into a very loud tone, clearly ready to stir things up.

"So, Tatiana—what do you think of Ellie's exhibition? Have you been?"

Taken out of her conversation, Tatiana looks around, irritated to be put on the spot in such an obvious way. She has seen Ellie's paintings online, but hasn't yet been to see the new exhibition live, which will now sound offensive.

"No, I haven't been to the gallery..." She shifts her eyes towards Ellie, "but I saw your art elsewhere. I admire it greatly."

Ellie blinks, seemingly flattered. Tatiana finds that slightly suspicious, since she is already known to be a very successful artist in the city, soon to open another exhibition. False humility tends to quickly annoy Tatiana, especially when everyone at the table has probably been to Ellie's current exhibition at the gallery.

"I think it's very... traditional," she adds, only as she said it realizing it might sound rude.

Apparently, she's not the only one to notice the ambiguous tone of her compliment. Everyone shifts on their seats, feeling the tense atmosphere rise in the air. Fred delights in it, believing that vigorous disagreements or misunderstandings lead to the most fruitful self-discoveries. He quietly begins collecting the dirty dishes from around the table, making room for dessert. Tatiana pours herself some more wine, slightly embarrassed.

"Hm... I do think I rely on tradition, since landscape paintings have such a rich history," Ellie gently remarks. "But Tatiana, you also rely on tradition."

I fucking don't.

"In what sense?" Tatiana asks, genuinely curious where Ellie is headed.

"Well, in order to subvert the form, you must have first learned its rules—no?"

"I definitely studied landscape painting in art school, but I rejected the romantic tradition, relying rather on my own imagination. Sometimes I paint what I see in nature."

As soon as she ends the sentence, Tatiana feels very proud of her own straightforwardness, having avoided the convoluted language Ellie seems to like using. The cold rim of the half-full wine glass strokes her lips, as she looks at Ellie's earrings dangling close to her bare neck. Her lovely bare neck. She takes a pensive sip of wine and the image of her kissing Ellie's lovely neck flickers unwantedly into her mind.

"I agree that we shouldn't think of what influences us while we paint," Ellie states enthusiastically, remembering the lessons her mother taught her, "but while painting, you necessarily use the tools you obtained beforehand. In school or otherwise."

"I think we strayed far from the original discussion," Tatiana says, feeling the little drops of wine tingle her teeth. She didn't like conversations to meander. "You say you're wary of contemporary art. Did you like my paintings?"

Tatiana notices a growing need in herself to hear Ellie's honest, raw critique. She's craving for Ellie to tear her art to shreds or proclaim it prophetic, no matter, she needs this woman's opinion. Something makes her crave it intensely. Perhaps it is Ellie's very thinly veiled confidence in her own opinions, perhaps it is the undoubted skill she puts into her own paintings. Tatiana leans in closer over the table to savor each word.

"I..." Ellie hesitates, but decides to continue, "I thought that your use of bold strokes and mismatched colors was captivating. It definitely made me reflect on your—the artist's—intentions, the reasons for, sometimes, going against the form and painting over it with such disregard." She nods to Tatiana, encouragingly. "But I also think the majority of your younger audience resonates with your art purely because it is *against the grain*. Or, not really against the current grain, but against the previous grain—which makes it follow the current one."

Tatiana, even though waiting for the last sentence to be a punch set up by the kind opening, still feels stung. She looks away, condemning herself for giving Ellie the blessing to be honest and failing to withstand it. *What kind of an artist cannot handle honest critique?* She rambles in her thoughts, seeing Fred carry dessert on little trays.

"I don't agree with your approach to art," Tatiana lashes out suddenly, speaking louder than before. "Not because I want to disregard tradition or because I disagree that *certain* contemporary art doesn't carry a lot of merit, but because through such a harsh stance on subverting form, you can easily discourage young, provocative artists."

Ellie straightens herself up on her chair, visibly touched. No one wants to discourage young artists, and such a harsh accusation certainly merits a harsh response. She thinks, but for too short a time, perhaps.

"I want to direct young artists and make sure their education gives them the tools to express their sensitivity and a critical approach towards art. That means welcoming various points of view, including ones that remain skeptical of *some* of your work, for example," Ellie finishes, taking a deep breath.

Tatiana's face flushes with heat. She wasn't expecting such a personal argument to unravel, but being a naturally stubborn person, she refuses to let this thread go. The entire table remains quiet, no one daring to interrupt the painters' discussion. Probably mainly for their own entertainment, feeling a particular sort of infatuation with the emotions playing on the two women's faces. Fred quietly distributed little plates of tiramisu during the heated exchange, and now both Ellie and Tatiana stare down at their portions, with no appetite left to eat.

"Which work, for example?" Presses Tatiana, having let a few moments pass.

"*The swing*. I don't like *The Swing*. I think that the splash of paint," Ellie stops for a split second, perhaps realizing that the three glasses of wine did their job, but choosing to continue regardless, "the splash of paint really just destroys the beautiful job you did crafting the hill landscape, even the swing itself is astonishing. So ethereal. And then the splash—"

"The splash is the swing. It is the essence of the painting," interrupts Tatiana, wanting to explain in haste, "otherwise it would've been just an old, uninteresting landscape. Like *some* of yours."

Take that, you uptight opinionated bitch!

Why am I thinking about the lovely way her waist dips below her breasts and then flares out into her hips?

Now the guests gasp, finally realizing they probably should have stopped such a personal argument from escalating. Thomas excuses himself to the bathroom, feeling awkward.

"Alright, alright, girls—" Fred cuts in as the host of the dinner, "we are all artists here, we all employ various techniques, there's no need to be so harsh to each other. I love both of your work. I wish you both the best," he continues, trying to remove some steam from the situation, somewhat clumsily. They look at him with friendly disregard.

"I wish Ellie all the best," Tatiana responds, "I just think that maybe we shouldn't be putting love letters in galleries."

Ellie laughs, animated, and her earrings glimmer, again stroking her neck.

Her long elegant pale neck that is begging for my lips on it. Stop it, Tatiana. It has been too long since you got laid. Clearly.

Tatiana turns her eyes away not to stare.

"Even *if* my art were a love letter to romanticism—which it is not—I think that putting love letters in galleries would be very much in the vein of contemporary art. I bet someone has done that already."

"You have so much potential and you refuse to channel it into something more creative, you refuse to let your work flow. It feels rigid. It feels contained," says Tatiana defiantly, getting up from her chair. "That's all I think."

"I'm almost forty," Ellie reminds her. "I have explored my potential well up to this point, I think. There is excellence to be found in something rigid. Like ballet."

"You know what—" Tatiana looks straight at Ellie, "I'll just go. I'm tired and I've had enough wine."

She makes her way to Fred, leaning in to say goodbye.

"Fred, thanks a lot for the invitation, I'm sorry about this." She makes an ambiguous gesture with her hands. "I left you a wine bottle in the corridor, I forgot."

"Don't worry," Fred laughs, walking her to the hallway. "Are you sure you can drive, though?"

She stops, one arm in her coat, remembering that she drove here in her car.

"Shit. Can I leave it here for now?" Her eyes bat

apologetically, knowing fully well that Fred has more than enough space to keep it.

"Pfft, sure. Don't get so heated with Ellie, please." Fred's tone changes to one that sounds very earnest, almost caring. "She treats her art very seriously, like all of us, but on top of that she can be very insecure."

Tatiana shakes her head, amused. There was not a tinge of insecurity in what she saw.

"Doesn't seem so to me, for sure," she remarks dismissively, buttoning up her coat.

"I'm serious," Fred picks up the purse that slid down Tatiana's shoulder. Ready to go, she gets back to the dining room to say goodbye to the sitting group.

"Bye everyone, I got very tired, as you could see—"

Kind laughter erupts around the table, omitting only Ellie. She nods at Tatiana, and possibly neither of them knows what it is supposed to mean.

"See you around!" Tatiana exclaims, trying to counter the still lingering unpleasant mood. Once out of the door, she breathes more easily.

—

Gentle taps of scarce raindrops hit the cab's roof. Tatiana sits in the backseat, reflecting on the afternoon, and with time, the waves of anger fade out from her chest. She catches sharp notes of disappointment playing around her thoughts; she was thinking that maybe the dinner would convince her to open herself up to Ellie's art. Instead, it only served to further their differences. Ellie's self-assured tone still rang about Tatiana's ears, causing a mixture of disapproval and a strange sense of inferiority she hadn't felt since college. Ellie, in Tatiana's mind, sounded almost cruel. Watching the cars go by and the rain grow thicker, she keeps circling back to the tinge of hope she felt when she thought that Ellie could approve of her paintings. Perhaps something of that beauty, contained in between her delicate pale skin and her golden jewelry and hair, could have seeped into Ellie's opinions. The softness of her voice would perhaps make them tender and under-standing. But it didn't. Instead, Tatiana was left bitter and curled on the cab's backseat, watching the promising spring weather of the day wash away, while thoughts of fucking Ellie Matthews until she shut up her stupid opinions flashing insistently through her head.

4

ELLIE

Having said all her goodbyes and hugged all of her newly acquired friends—even Marceline, for by the end of the evening, they made peace—Ellie spilled out of the house onto the rain-showered streets. She had taken a bus to Fred's but feeling the rain-freshened air bloom in her lungs, she decides to walk back home. Her mind feels swollen with thoughts and remnants of alcohol, but each step replenishes her clarity of thought, lifting her spirits up as well. For now, she refuses to think, only taking deep breaths, knowing that the avalanche of reflections will befall her soon enough.

Somewhere in the middle of the way, she

remembers Tatiana Khan's shattered expression upon hearing the blunt criticism of *The Swing,* blown out of proportion. The image of Tatiana's muddy-brown eyes looking from across the table with disappointment and hurt stirs something within Ellie, maybe even regret.

Tatiana had been much more attractive than Ellie had imagined. Her shimmering red hair had made Ellie want to capture it on canvas, it was like no color she had ever seen before.

She shakes her head to reject the image, reminding herself that she only spoke her mind. *Artists should be able to handle critique,* she keeps reminding herself, jumping over puddles of water like a little child. The streets observe her with a quiet emptiness.

And Tatiana might have been beautiful, but she was still an arrogant pain in the ass.

The truth is, Ellie really dislikes the bolder paintings of Tatiana Khan. What surprised her during the argument, however, was Tatiana's insistence on Ellie's unoriginality. She has, naturally, heard before that her paintings weren't exciting, but that is a sentiment commonly encountered by landscape artists.

Nonetheless, she has always thought that her

paintings remained imbued with a tenderness and sensitivity, especially open to be perceived by other artists. Now, she almost feels betrayed. The silence around the two didn't help either, making Ellie think that the others agreed with Tatiana's point. To shake away the irritating thoughts, she decides to stop by a particularly inviting perfume store and buy herself a beautifully smelling treat.

"What scents do you prefer, Ma'am?" The bored saleswoman is quick to jump from her desk, seeing Ellie enter.

"Something fresh. Citrusy, for sure," Ellie smiles, eyeing the little bottles.

She ends up purchasing a lemon zest & cinnamon fragrance, perfect in her mind, to welcome spring. Perfume has always been an important part of her personality, and an unfortunately expensive tool to cope with unpleasant emotions.

With the newly purchased scent in her purse, she decides to make the rest of the way by bus, feeling her legs grow tired. The affair with Tatiana still rattling around her mind, she hears her phone ring.

"Yes?" She picks up.

"Hi! It's Emma, I'm calling to remind you about your exhibition opening in three days?"

Ellie chuckles a bit at the thought that she could somehow forget such an important event, nonetheless grateful for the reminder.

"Hi Emma, thanks a lot. Are there any new important guests, guests I don't know about?"

Emma pauses for a bit, and Ellie can hear her exhale into the phone.

"Yes... Actually. Margaret said she would show up."

The news tightens Ellie's chest, a grief worked over and healed, all the same present. She sits down at a nearby bench, waiting for her bus to arrive. She hasn't seen Margaret in a year and was not really expecting her to show up out of nowhere.

"Alright, well. She is a part of the art world, and we're on civil terms," says Ellie rationally, though little needles of anxiety sting her lungs.

"Great, you have all the details in your mail-box," summarizes Emma. "See you there?"

"See you there. Make sure to go over everything twice." And having said so, Ellie hangs up.

Her complex feelings for Margaret manage to

eclipse her grievances related to Tatiana for the duration of the bus ride. Her old love, always a difficult person, could be a true challenge to manage during events. Getting off on her street and standing in front of the front door, however, Ellie decides to cast all the worries aside for the night.

She prepares chamomile tea and plays French New Wave films, for a moment silently criticizing herself for procrastinating her French lessons. Bundled up, she lets the melodic language carry her troubling feelings, and finally, enveloped by her thick blanket, she drifts away to sleep somehow unable to completely get thoughts of Tatiana bloody Khan and her shimmering red hair and full lips out of her head.

5

TATIANA

The intestines of her wardrobe seemed to spill out onto her in the most chaotic of ways. Tatiana rummaged through her clothes, trying to think of the most creative and flattering of combinations, failing miserably. She had a particularly violent love-hate relationship with getting ready to attend events; on the one hand feeling attracted by the glamour of dressing up, on the other always procrastinating until the very last minute. Finally, she decides to call Connie.

"You need to help me," she cries, in between two suits and three dresses. "I have tons of clothes, I don't think any look good, I need to leave in three hours, and I still haven't done my make-up or hair," she spits out in one breath.

"Three hours is a lot of time," Connie laughs. "What's the big deal about this? You go to these events a few times a week, sometimes."

Tatiana freezes, side-tracked. She hasn't questioned why this opening, Ellie's opening, put so much pressure on her. She simply caved in, accepting that for this evening she must look like a god, or muse. She wants to look powerful, self-assured, and of good taste.

"It's this Ellie Matthews," she explains, trying on another shirt, "we argued about each other's art, and she said some pretty rude things. I want to look good to spite her, I guess."

Or because I want to fuck her?

The shirt looks disproportionate and lands on the quickly growing pile of unacceptable clothing.

"How is that even connected in your mind?" inquiries Connie, slowly giving up on the thread.

Tatiana doesn't answer, whirling around her bedroom, growing desperate.

"Listen," Connie lights up suddenly, "remember that suit you wore a month ago to Gustav's concert? It looked so good on you. And the blouse you wore made it very androgynous, kind of hot."

"Kind of hot?"

"Very hot."

After hanging up, Tatiana decides to go with Connie's advice and wear the androgynous, hot suit. What feels like hours of ironing, finally makes the suit and the blouse acceptable.

On the way, she's surprised to realize that she will make it on time. The traffic is light, and the sky is without a single cloud. Soon enough, the stars will richly pepper the sky. Tatiana feels a rush of excitement that always comes to her with artistic events. The vibrant crowd attending these never fails to sweep her up in some fruitful conversation, the drinks are always free, and she feels on top of the world, knowing that often the parties are invite-only. It's exactly what she dreamt of, choosing to attend art school.

Tatiana enters the modern building, shiny and the color of bone. Its imposing pillars stretch tall, sturdy. She has always thought it to be designed particularly beautifully—even though simple, through its shape and materials it conveys a sort of ancient authority, reminiscent of Greek architecture. The long, wide staircase leads her into the main hall, already half-full, bustling with conversation. Along the walls are Ellie's paintings, though not yet lit up. It seems to be quite a collection. She catches her own reflection in a mirror and flashes a smile, feeling particularly good about the way she looks tonight, her bright red hair shining in long strings, reflecting the strong, artificial light.

Finally, she can see someone get on the small stage and introduce Ellie. The introduction remains brief and contained, which she appreciates. There is nothing worse for Tatiana than a lengthy, self-absorbed introduction, knowing that the artists usually write them themselves anyway. She has to admit, Ellie looks radiant in her dark green dress, reminiscent of the jade stones found in old jewels. Her golden hair is embellished by golden pins, twinkling in Tatiana's eyes.

"Good evening." Ellie seems to be nervous, looking around the audience. "I want to begin by thanking you all for coming, but a few people in particular..."

Hearing the welcome, Tatiana slowly, unintentionally, drifts away. She knows these speeches by heart and having no mind to pay attention to Ellie's words, she tunes into her calming voice. It flows like an ocean, tides licking the sand of her ears. For a moment, she shifts her attention onto the crowd, looking for familiar faces. She manages to spot Fred and Thomas, appearing exquisite in their matching suits, electric red. There are many acquaintances of hers here that she fell out of touch with or don't talk to often, and a bunch of fresh, new faces. She listens in just as Ellie gets to the end of the lengthy formal introduction, full of gratefulness.

"Now, before I let you roam around and explore the works for yourselves, I wanted to give you brief context for these. This series of land-scapes in particular is very personal to me, but in an unusual manner. As some of you may know, I'm very close with my family. Their never-ending support is what brought me here in the first place, I could never commit to my career without them. My mother and my father both influenced my creativity from the earliest age, but tonight I want to shift the focus onto my lovely sister, Alexandra. Recently we've been drifting further apart, but we still manage to call once in a while. Whenever we call, she likes to tell me about her dreams. Ladies and gentlemen, these are the landscapes of my sister's dreams—"

The audience claps, and Tatiana joins in, sincerely quite enchanted by the idea.

"When I first began sketching them, I didn't think much of it. Later, however, I tried matching what I sketched with real places, finding much aesthetic satisfaction. Blending the elements into paintings evolved into the collection you can see now."

Just as she finished the last sentence, the paintings lit up. Against the dark, ruby walls, the delicate pastels of Ellie's landscapes provide a gentle respite for the eye. Tatiana comes up to the one closest, expecting to see this dreamy, unreal quality she imagined while Ellie was speaking. Her mind busies itself with the wonderful potential such a project has, but it all comes to a halt when she sees the most tame of landscapes. There is nothing in it to suggest a land of dreams, and she grows annoyed. She grows disillusioned with the conventions that still seem to tie together the art world.

She decides to look for the bathroom to take a break from the increasingly hot crowd, swarming around the images in large groups. On her way, she catches a glimpse of Ellie talking to a particularly elevated woman. The woman's clothes, a bold, checkered dress with a matching jacket scream *glamorous*, complimented by her vibrant red lips. She looks spectacular. Soon, however, Tatiana loses them out of sight and enters the spacious bathroom. The tiles look polished to the extreme, white with ruby elements.

The cold water splashes on Tatiana's hands, and while she's applying the lavender-scented soap, she can see Ellie walk in, reflected in the mirror facing her. At first, Ellie doesn't seem to notice Tatiana, preoccupied by something. Her dress touches the floor, rustling quietly with movement. She splashes water on her face, sighing heavily. Little droplets stick to her forehead, dropping to her eyelashes. Upon raising her face to begin fixing her makeup in the mirror, she at last crosses eyes with Tatiana. They look at each other, at a bit of a loss for words. Tatiana has clearly been observing Ellie, and they both stand aware of the fact.

"Everything alright?" Tatiana finally asks.

"Sure." Ellie shrugs, smiling a bit smug. "I'm glad you came to see the opening. How do you like the paintings?"

Ellie's shoulders stand softly bare under the cold bathroom light, her neck endearingly ornamented with one, single pearl. The pearl fits exactly in between her collarbones, moving up and down with the subtle tides of her breathing.

"I like them," Tatiana says, nodding to herself.

Why can't I stop fantasising about fucking her?

Not knowing what to say next, she feels oppressed by the intimacy of being with Ellie alone in an empty room. Her feet urge her to go, so she picks up her purse and leaves.

On her way back to the paintings, she feels burning annoyance grow in her chest. The heavy sensation keeps reminding her of her strange behavior, clearly quite rude. She has no explanation for her brisk response, besides the fact that she really dislikes the paintings. The wasted potential of the concept keeps getting on her nerves, and passing from frame to frame, she picks up a glass of champagne. The refreshing liquid slides down her throat pleasantly, with a gentle bubbling.

"Tatiana!" Fred calls to her, quite tipsy and joyful. "I adore it; I'm fascinated by her idea."

"As if you two haven't been talking about these paintings for months prior," Tatiana smiles, looking at his genuine excitement.

"Don't tell me you think this isn't brilliant." He steps back.

Tatiana looks around the hall, taking in the

paintings. She can see the craft, the skill, the endearing little boats floating atop seas of dreams. When she thinks that these truly represent someone's dreaming state, a landscape woven out of someone's morning recollections, she shivers with admiration. What disturbs her is that she could easily confuse these with any other landscape paintings. Especially the ones closer to impressionism, perhaps, the soft edges and pastel colors reminiscent of the style. Nonetheless, they looked like any other lake, any other sea. The meaning, in her opinion, was not well translated.

"I... Honestly, I don't think she managed to convey the idea well," Tatiana admits, still looking at the painting facing them.

Fred waves her away, dismissively shaking his head.

"Girl, you're just obsessed with critiquing Ellie's art. Admit it. It's good."

"It's good." Tatiana nods. "It fails to be *great*."

They part ways, each called to different parts of the hall. Tatiana shortly meets Marceline, but their conversation feels fragmented and inconsistent, so each makes up an excuse to drift away back into the crowd. Tatiana admires the young Marceline greatly, but they tend to gravitate towards very different spheres, she recently noticed. Putting her empty glass back on the tray, she contemplates drinking another one. The golden bubbles swim up, defying gravity. An appealing invitation she nonetheless decides to postpone.

Out of the crowd of voices Tatiana gradually untangles the thread of Ellie's, so singularly deep. She seems to be nearby, probably somewhere in the back.

"I'm not complaining. I just wasn't expecting you to come, that's all." She sounds on the edge, distracted. Tatiana's curiosity builds up, forever insatiable. She has always been an incorrigible eavesdropper, catching and sewing together scattered fragments of hushed conversations.

"Well, I'm sorry for driving a ton of people to see your exhibition. Won't do it again," the other voice scoffs.

Tatiana turns to look for the pair, finding Ellie once more with the checkered-dress woman. There seems to be some unspoken grief between them, but catching Ellie's glance, she turns her head away.

Going from acquaintance to acquaintance making small talk, Tatiana grows impatient to have a longer conversation with Ellie, eager to remedy the clumsy bathroom one. She feels peculiarly unresolved when it comes to their relations, and ideally, she would like to straighten things out. She doesn't like to think of herself as uncivil, or ill-educated. Worse yet, someone who can't stomach criticism.

She caves into the temptation and downs another glass of champagne, preparing to go looking for the artist of the night, hunting for a glimpse of her dress. Asking around she finds nothing, at this point during the evening the guests tied themselves into neat groups, disinterested in others. Hopeless, she finally spots the dark green dress somewhere near, quickly following. She finds Ellie drinking water in a secluded corner, next to the bathrooms. The weight of these events can sometimes take its toll on an artist, putting themselves out there to be judged. Approaching, Tatiana realizes she's entirely unsure of the course she wants the conversation to take, unsure even of what she means to say.

She looks so beautiful. Emerald dress. Emerald eyes.

"Hey." She takes a place next to Ellie, leaning in against the wall.

"Hey, Tatiana," Ellie looks at her. "I heard you don't like my paintings," she sighs. The sentence doesn't come out as hurt or offended, rather quite playful.

"No, I don't mean—" Tatiana gets flustered, mad at Fred for sharing such a raw opinion.

"That's okay," Ellie interrupts her. "I got to exhibit either way, didn't I?"

She tilts her head to the side, and the rich storm of her golden hair embraces her face in an effortless compliment. There is something tired about her eyes, Tatiana cannot guess what exactly, but she can still see a playful sparkle swirl around in their depth. She sobers up, looking away.

"Well, that's just arrogant," she says in blank disbelief.

"You have that effect, don't you? I want to be blunt with you," Ellie fires back.

The women look at each other, soaking in the honesty of such a raw confession. Tatiana doesn't know what to do with her limbs, suddenly awkwardly aware of her arms. She crosses them on her chest, unluckily taking on a more assertive pose. They stand face to face, hugged by the wall's support.

"I think that the idea is more powerful than the art. That's my honest opinion," she decides to get it out, thinking that perhaps being straightforward is the best solution. They're both artists of their own right, allowed to critique each other, constructively. She licks her lips, dried out in the hall's crowded air. The dry skin, covered by her lipstick, stings.

"You just bash my art every time we talk," Ellie nods. "I have no strength for this tonight, frankly" she says, leaning in closer. "I'm tired."

"Why are you tired?" Tatiana says more quietly, now that the distance between them diminished so abruptly. She loses her focus.

The conversation has its own tracks, but confronted with the naked reality of Ellie's neck, Tatiana's body enters a different form of dialogue. Their arms dance around each other, careful not to collide, but careful not to get too far away. Tatiana's nostrils flutter, tingled by notes of lemons and cinnamon, mingled with the heat of Ellie's body. She keeps failing to decide where to keep her eyes, sliding around Ellie's collarbones, lips, finally her eyes.

"There's a very demanding guest here tonight," Ellie admits, seeming equally distracted. She looks to the floor, and Tatiana can swear her cheeks appear more vibrant than usual.

"The woman in the checkered dress," Tatiana lets out slowly, pronouncing every syllable. They roll off her tongue like candy, each word full and round. "Am I right?"

Ellie gives her a prolonged look, her gaze sliding down Tatiana's eyes towards her lips. She gets closer, and tall as she is, forces Tatiana to look up at her.

"I don't want to be talking about that woman," she whispers in a husky voice, close to Tatiana's ear, sending filaments of shivers up her back, weakening her knees a little bit.

Tatiana looks around, slightly ashamed to discover her legs itching to part. Ellie stands so close that the heat of her body strokes her skin, and even little breaths can be felt, raising the net of goosebumps around Tatiana's body.

"What do you want to talk about?" Tatiana swallows a bit loudly, keeping her gaze up.

Ellie raises her hand, her fingers wrapped by heavy rings make their gentle way up and down Tatiana's throat, stroking her delicate skin. Tatiana leans in closer, enchanted and hot, desire now in full swing in her mind, pumping her boiling blood with force.

Ellie's lips raise their corners in a little smile, seeing her thirsty eyes. She leans in, sticking her tongue out and tracing Tatiana's lips.

"Kiss me," Tatiana whispers, impatient and in a feverish state of want.

"Well not here," Ellie clicks her tongue, looking around. "But if you go with me to the bathroom... I'll fuck you the way you deserve it."

Oh, fuck. Yes.

The sudden force of her voice sends a wave down Tatiana's legs. Now she really wants to get fucked like she deserves it, whatever that may be in Ellie's mind. She can feel her heartbeat pulsing in her neck, her thoughts overflowing with dirty imaginings. There was nothing about Ellie that prepared her for this, she thought at first, but now she understands. The comprehension fills up her mind, making her hungry to hear more.

A bit dazed, she looks around, takes Ellie's hand, and sneakily leads her to the bathroom. She feels like a teenager again, an insolent brat about to get in trouble. The thought only makes Ellie's promise more appealing.

They enter and the bathroom stands empty, in its full invitation to commit something salacious. Ellie closes the door behind them, and grabs Tatiana closer to her.

"So, you don't appreciate my art?" she demands, distractingly close to Tatiana's face.

"Ellie—" Tatiana begins, confused, but is quickly interrupted.

"Don't lie to me," Ellie shakes her head slowly. "Let's play," she smiles.

A smile slowly forms on Tatiana's face as well, finally comprehending to the fullest their situation. If there is tension to be played out, so be it. She can feel her underwear get moist only thinking of Ellie's voice in her ear.

"I don't appreciate it," Tatiana admits, nodding.

"You'll appreciate something else, then," says Ellie. "Are you ready to get fucked, darling?"

Tatiana's mouth goes dry. The words ring in her ears. She certainly wasn't expecting the exhibition to turn out this way, but she isn't going to deny herself the pleasure now. She always imagined herself fucking Ellie, but this sudden twist of events, she can certainly get on board with.

"Yes, I am," she responds, compliant.

"Good," Ellie looks down at her. "Keep being good then, and go to the stall."

"Are you serious?"

"Very serious," Ellie says, stroking Tatiana's neck once more. She traces her jawline, finally slipping two fingers in her mouth. "Go now."

So Tatiana does, walking into the nearby tight

bathroom stall. Her breathing gets shallow and fast, waiting for Ellie to join her. After a moment Ellie enters the stall, looking Tatiana up and down. She unzips Tatiana's pants, sliding them down. Her hand wanders in between Tatiana's thighs, feeling the wet mess of her lacy underwear and nodding. She slides that down as well.

"See? You're so pretty when you're not being rude," she teases. "Now turn around."

Tatiana does what she's told, almost shivering. The honey drops of Ellie's voice make her spread her legs a bit wider with each command, unsure what's going to happen next, but excited for everything. There's nothing in her mind now other than Ellie's touch, her words, her breath on Tatiana's skin.

"Wider, and bend over slightly," Ellie instructs patiently, laying her hand on Tatiana's ass.

Tatiana spreads her legs wider and reaches the wall, feeling her blouse lift up, exposing her entirely. The tense suspense makes her legs tremble, she tries to tame them but fails.

She feels Ellie's arms wrap around her legs, and she is aware of Ellie sinking to the floor behind her.

"You're so wet for me, dear," she observes, smirking.

She can feel Ellie's breath hot against her pussy and it almost blows her mind.

Her tongue traces Tatiana's vulva gently up and down, preparing to have her. When she starts eating Tatiana out properly, there is no mercy left. Her tongue licks up and down with a challenging but steady tempo, pressure applied just right. Tatiana's hips soon start grinding, craving more violent pleasure, craving to show how much she wants it. Ellie's tongue swirls round, and back and forth. A little moan escapes Tatiana's lips—

"Shh. Be quiet," Ellie reminds, having to stop working her.

"I'm sorry," Tatiana manages to utter, desperate to get it back. She bites her lips and shuts her eyes.

Once back at it, Ellie begins entering Tatiana with her tongue, precise and strong. She stops, gently slapping her ass.

"Now you'll get what you deserve," she says, getting back up on her feet.

"What?" asks Tatiana, her mind half lost to the rhythm of her hips.

"I'll have you all stretched out for me, praying you

could moan. Here in this public bathroom, baby," Ellie whispers into Tatiana's ear and Tatiana hears the clang of metal which she assumes is Ellie taking her rings off before sliding a finger into her from behind.

"Yes please," Tatiana manages to say, before she has to seal her mouth shut.

Ellie picks up the pace and Tatiana feels multiple fingers pushing inside of her, stretching her wide, and soon, Tatiana's thoughts evaporate. She knows this is what she wanted desperately.

Against the cold tiles of the bathroom wall, she's clenching her fists, turning her head back to look at Ellie, pushing her ass higher and trying not to cry out as Ellie's fingers fuck her hard and fast, pressing downwards at her G spot. It feels more incredible than she can ever remember any other sex feeling, this hot dirty toilet cubicle sex.

"More.. please..." she hears herself whimper and doesn't recognise her own voice.

"Oh, baby, I thought you would never ask," Ellie growls in her ear. A handful of Tatiana's hair is tight in Ellie's left hand while her right hand begins to push. Ellie is pushing more inside of Tatiana, more fingers, all of her fingers, opening her up and stretching her, so she will be taken absolutely by Ellie. Tatiana wants it so much.

She feels Ellie's hand pressuring to get inside of her and she pushes her ass back against it, desperate to take Ellie's whole hand inside her soaking wet pussy.

She feels the pressure heighten some more, for just a few seconds and she's not sure she can bare it any longer and then suddenly, relief as her whole hand slides inside.

Fuck.

"Oh god, Yes." Tatiana knows she is no longer being quiet as Ellie begins to slowly but surely rock Tatiana on her fist.

It feels exquisite and she can feel Ellie's knuckles pressing her G spot. She knows she is very very close.

Ellie begins to fuck her slow and deep with her whole hand.

"Come on, come now for me, Tatiana."

"Can I?" she gasps, strained.

The pressure feels just right, insufferably so. Ellie's hand is like a pump, forcing into her a state of unendurable ecstasy.

"Of course." Ellie is as smug as ever and even now, Tatiana hates her.

But this, this exquisite fucking, this fisting of

her, this takeover of her body; it feels so very very good.

And she does what she's told, coming hard again and again, her orgasm gushing down the insides of her thighs. She hears herself crying out in ecstasy with Ellie's hand deep inside.

—

Disentangled, they sit on the bathroom floor in a short-lived silent bliss. Ellie gets up to wash her hands, watching for stains on her dress—fortunate to find none. She begins sliding her gold rings back on. Soon, knocking on the bathroom door interrupts them, reminding them both of the absurdity of their situation.

"Ellie! Are you there? People are looking for you," Fred shouts through the thick barrier. He's audibly tipsy, loudly laughing to someone else.

"Yes! I'm coming," Ellie quickly fixes herself in the mirror and rushes out of the bathroom. She doesn't cast even a glance in Tatiana's direction, only clutching her purse close.

Tatiana is left standing next to the stall, confused about what just happened. She washes her face, trying to grasp that the encounter was real, attempting to mute the little fluttering of her heart at the thought of Ellie's hands. The conversation clearly failed, not making their relationship any less convoluted. She feels the now-cold wet lace in between her thighs.

What the fuck, she thinks, picking up her things and looking for an excuse to tell everyone in order to avoid the afterparty. She drinks some of the tap water and leaves the bathroom. The crowd engulfs her, and the ruby walls seem suffocating. Home is calling.

Her car stands loyally where she left it, for once easy to find. She throws her purse inside and takes the seat, still in a state of cluttered disbelief. *In a bathroom stall,* she shakes her head, thinking back to high school. She turns on the radio and lets it drown out her tangled thoughts. Soon, her mind seems to enter a quiet sort of flow induced by the monotony of driving and the radio hosts' voices. She lets her mind roam free, sometimes memories or observations resurface, causing her to smirk, then pause, then smirk again.

I can still feel her hand inside of me.

6

ELLIE

The softness kissing Ellie's forehead refuses to let her slip away from dreams. Her mind feels hot and gooey, sticky fragments of thoughts intertwined with dreams mill around her head. Dreary clouds, hanging heavy outside the window, dim all morning light. This cloud-induced sleepy atmosphere in the room ties her to the bed even further. She twists her head left to right, slowly making peace with the need to face the day's reality. Getting up has never been her strength, especially after difficult nights.

Brushing her teeth, Ellie plays the memory of sex with Tatiana Khan over and over again, like a washing machine inept at its job. The memory becomes no less dirty, no less confusing, no less intimidating. She spits the toothpaste out into the sink, creating a nasty stain.

What the fuck, she thinks, remembering the bathroom stall.

For breakfast, she decides to make a three-egg omelette with spinach and garlic, her sister's favorite morning dish. When life presents her with difficult situations, she resorts to making easy decisions, choices she can be certain in. This way, she keeps up the sense of control and stability she always craves—and always seems to forsake in her relationships with women. *That's the problem,* she thinks, flipping the omelette. She knows what she wants, the mature woman that she is, and she knows what she can give. But somehow, she gets infatuated with these chaotic thunderstorms of women. Margaret...

That memory stings too much, and she gently lets it go.

Sprinkling salt and pepper into the pan, she rewinds the evening to before the intimate act. *It's good. It's not great,* keeps playing in her thoughts, a stinging reality to be confronted with. The overheard conversation with Fred upset Ellie more than anything else Tatiana had said before, upset and angered her at the same time. There was no reason for Ellie to accept Tatiana's authority regarding anything. Especially because Tatiana's art itself was not to Ellie's liking, she repeated this idea to herself to no avail.

Sitting down to have her breakfast, she resolves to at last visit Tatiana's exhibition before going to meet her father. She has been looking forward to seeing him for weeks now, their phone calls sparse and unfulfilling. His health is not the best either, she has recently learned.

Circling back to Tatiana, she supposes that giving her art a fair chance seems a reasonable thing to do. Perhaps the paintings look better live. But truth be told, she doesn't even want to like them anymore—she grew comfortable in her line of critique. The thought of the landscapes upsets her, even.

Why was fucking her so satisfying? Fucking her contempt for my art out of her. Opening her up to take all of me. Hearing her moan for me, cry for me, come for me.

Then leaving her, wet and spent in a bathroom cubicle.

Her pussy felt so good around my hand.

Stop it, Ellie. It was a mistake.

Finishing up, she looks out the window, let down by having to take out her woolen sweater again. Those days were supposed to be past already, their cold and grey attitude affects Ellie, and also means worse light in her studio. Not wanting to work under artificial light, she has been particularly excited for the sunny days, the paintings she can create, inspired by the spring.

She gets in her car, even though recently she has been feeling a strange aversion towards driving. Behind the wheel, every thought seems to be able to sleaze around her mind infinitely; memories, dreams, and fragments of conversations stumble in and out of her train of thought. She can't wait to talk to her father, who always manages to take her thoughts into his gentle palms and straighten them out. He's always been able to do that, throughout her teenage years especially. Years wrought with confusion and getting constantly lost, figuring out her own identity. When she said she might like women, he was the most supportive person in her life, together with her mother.

She had been lucky.

—

It's not a bad gallery, she admits, on her arrival. She has been here before, five or six years ago, to see another rising artist. His linoleum art made a true impression on her back then, unfortunately his career came to a halt, and she didn't hear much about him afterwards. Leaving her coat in the cloakroom, she enters the space currently empty of visitors except herself. Sustaining herself purely as an artist, she likes the freedom to move around the city when most people are at work.

The paintings exhibited here vary in style; she can see that Tatiana's earlier paintings are hung around the walls, as well as the most recent ones. There remains a common thread of splashing vibrances, jarring colors clashing or mingling with each other against the backdrop of landscapes, sometimes incorporated into them, though rarely. Tatiana's earlier work seems less coherent, though Ellie finds a particularly interesting painting.

Below stormy clouds, mingled with the sea appear pools and boiling splashes of bold, red blood, storming together with the forces of nature. Lightning bolts spin their thin white scars along the dark sky, and looking at it, Ellie can almost hear the thunder. Apocalyptic though it is, Ellie is entirely captivated by the pure emotion of the piece, as well as its skillful execution. It's called *Sacrifice and* was painted four years ago.

Ellie stands there, transfixed by the painting. She could easily admit it to be Tatiana's best work, so different from what she focuses on creating now. The blood seems well incorporated into the piece, in theory taking place within it, even though appearing mythically out of the realm of the storm. She looks at other paintings, disapproving of some, and admitting that others are not as bad. Looking at the time she hurries to the cloakroom, not wanting to be late for her meeting.

Sacrifice stays with Ellie the whole way back, down the galleries numerous steps, on the way to her car, and driving to the coffee shop. She feels curiosity rise within her; what inspired such a raw and unsettling painting? She feels that Tatiana could be better than she is, if she would rely less on the boldness of her pieces alone. The ones placed within the soft realm of ambiguity, in Ellie's opinion, are the ones which leave the most impact on the viewer, allowing one to dive into the piece entirely.

Once out of the car, she notices her father standing on the pavement in front of the coffee shop, smoking a pipe. A *nasty old habit,* he used to say, wanting to discourage his daughters from smoking.

"Dad!" She waves to him, almost brought to tears by how much older he looks now. His fragile frame stands engulfed in an old tweed jacket, and his dark complexion contrasts more and more sharply with the silver devouring his rich curls. She still has a little picture of him in her wallet from the time she was twenty, departing for college.

"Ellie, sweetheart!" He smiles wide, embracing her in his arms. "How're you doing?"

"Lots to talk about," she admits, leading him into the lively coffee shop.

They order and sit down by the window, beaming with joy to see each other again. Ellie sets her bag on the floor and having heard all the medical updates about her mother, sighs heavily.

"She's going to be alright, really," her father says, trying to cheer her up. "The doctors are very hopeful."

"I know, I know." Ellie nods. "She's a strong woman."

Their coffee arrives, steaming and milky.

"But tell me something about how you're doing," he urges.

Ellie takes her cup and decides to talk about her stormy feelings about Tatiana's art, omitting the bathroom incident, naturally.

Why did fucking her feel so good?

—

"So the way I see it," says Ellie's father, having listened to the story, "both of you dislike something about one another. One another's art," he corrects. "But maybe, it's really a different feeling."

"Like what?" Ellie leans in, always eager to listen to advice.

"I don't know. Envy, jealousy. You name it." Her father takes a long sip from his steaming cup, not a single trace of rush in his movements.

"I just think she's wasting the potential she has," Ellie continued, "I saw some other paintings of hers today, and one in particular... I really think it would be good for her to reflect more on her style, is all."

"So you like her?" He laughs, entertained. "You want to help her."

"I don't know what to think about her. She can be very mean." Ellie looks away. "I told you that."

Each time Ellie talks about Tatiana, she's

brought to the point of mingling the personal and the artistic, which begins annoying her. She annoys herself, really, always trying to stay in one track but soon bending over to the other. She wants to talk about Tatiana's art philosophy alone yet ends up grieving over her personality.

"It's always easier to like people," her father says pensively. "If you're unsure, choose love. Really, sometimes it's that simple. Especially among artists, you have to be understanding."

He takes out a sturdy, wooden box of chess from behind the table.

"Look," he says with a bright smile. "Should we?"

They play, winning interchangeably until they get bored and realize they've been sitting in the cafe far too long. Ellie goes up to the register to pay, returning in her thoughts to her father's advice.

"There's another side to this," she says, getting back to him. "I think I'm very insecure about my style next to her," she sighs. "Which is ridiculous, I mean, considering how long I've been doing this. I'm so much older and more experienced than her."

Her father shakes his head.

"What are you insecure about? People love your art, look at the two exhibitions you recently opened."

"Yes, but I recently started painting something new, and it really seems influenced by Tatiana Khan. I don't know how to feel about that, letting my art be so fragile."

They get outside, welcomed by a pleasant breeze. Ellie's father gestures to the nearby park, offering a walk before they part.

"Maybe you're not letting your art be fragile," he says after a while, "maybe you're letting it be flexible? You know, life lies in being able to bend and change form, stiff things are dead things."

"Maybe you're right, I shouldn't overthink it," she agrees.

The park grows crowded with children after school and young workers having their lunch breaks. The overall ambience is particularly joyful, play and laughter enveloping Ellie and her father in a pleasant atmosphere. Their steps remain unrushed, savoring the blissfully calm moment together. Unfortunately, the evening before keeps weighing her down.

"I think I do rush things when stressed," she confesses. Her throat feels tight.

"Don't we all," her father laughs. "Did something happen?"

"I um.. well.. had sex with Tatiana yesterday, and I don't know where that leads us, or where I want it to lead us."

"Oh!" He stops for a moment. "Well, that's complicated. At least it explains a lot of things between you two."

"I think I should take a break from all this and just focus on my painting," Ellie finally decides.

"If that's what you think you need, that's what you should do," her father agrees.

—

She drives him to his train station, telling him in detail about the exhibition's reception and how well regarded it is by critics. All that praise got eclipsed by Tatiana's scorn, unjustly, she realizes. How easy it is to let a single negative thing overshadow her hard work.

"Tell Alexandra to be proud," she smiles, "she's a part of the project."

They say their goodbyes and promise to see each other again soon. Ellie misses painting around her childhood home, where there is plenty of beautiful nature and landscapes only waiting to be captured by an observant eye. She's been thinking of acquiring a house somewhere in the area, perhaps when she's older. To have her own family settled among the lakes and forests of her youth.

Once her father disappears into the building, she contemplates driving to the studio. Seeing the cloudy sky, however, she heads home, on her way buying baskets of flowers. She misses the natural environment of her home, feeling separated from nature in the city, where every green patch seems scarce and unwelcoming. The parks seem tame and miserably small compared to the grand forests only a few minutes away from her old house. Perhaps the quiet force of nature imbued her paintings with the same kind of sensitivity, making her question the necessity of the screaming boldness she sometimes encounters within her contemporary peers. She begins suspecting that Tatiana, having grown up here, in the city, learned its violent language. Ellie wonders about her heritage as well, how it influenced the way she developed artistically. Perhaps for her, and where she has come from, the delicate expression stands as more revolutionary. In her art, she allows her brushstrokes to be gentle, unlike the course her life may have taken.

Having arrived at this thought, she decides to abandon the bold sketches of waterfalls.

Why can't I stop thinking about her?

7

TATIANA

Having avoided the sticky subject of Ellie Matthews for the whole day, Tatiana finally sits down to paint. Picking out the brushes, her thoughts slowly, quietly, settle down on the tracks leading towards the passionately avoided subject. Ellie's hand—she took all her gold rings off and then...

"Now you'll get what you deserve."

Oh my god...

She shakes her head, attempting to focus instead on her art, but to no avail. Last night is begging, low on its knees, to be touched. Tatiana runs her hand through her disarrayed hair, gazing blankly at the half-filled canvas. It's the sketch she made some time ago coming to life as a painting, the river banks filled by gentle colors stand ready as background, waiting to be completed. The longer Tatiana looks at her work, the more accusatory its glance appears. It is a dead thing looking back at her.

Feeling in no reasonable headspace to create, she gets up to make some coffee, dragging herself towards the kitchen. Opening the fridge, however, she realizes she hasn't bought any milk, having to abandon the idea—black coffee depresses her spirits. Resigned, she reaches for her phone, always a delectable distraction from any worry. Something nudges her to give Ellie's new exhibition another look, even though the subject clamors in her mind with a pulsing, swollen nervousness. She caves in.

Looking through the gallery of the event, she slowly sinks into herself. The paintings she scorned so much are not half as bad as she remembers them to be. Their somber ambience calls to the viewer with a siren-like appeal, well fitting for a dream landscape. Tatiana knits her eyebrows together, thoroughly searching for the reason for her aggravated state last night. Her opinions wriggle like live fish caught in the net of inconsistency, struggling and squirming to stay alive, confronted with the harshness of breathing. She desperately doesn't want to admit her mistake, even to herself, yet she cannot find many conceptual or technical faults within Ellie's numerous paintings. Their only possible flaw could be blandness, perhaps. But she doesn't want to go down that road, leading to nowhere. She turns the phone off, bitter.

The lack of milk upsets her but craving something cozy, she settles for milk-less tea. Waiting for the water to boil, the images of last night show up. They come in bursts, little fireworks of memories plaguing her mind. Ellie's soft voice rings in her ears, restless and menacing.

"Come now for me, Tatiana."

Tatiana doesn't want to think about what they did, and feeling hopelessly tangled up in her thoughts, she decides to reach out to an old friend. They were supposed to reconnect for a long time now, but each having their own constant professional hurdles to jump over, neither made the time to reach out.

"Marcel?" she says into the phone, hope dancing around her voice.

"Hey! Haven't heard from you in a long time!"

He sounds sunny like usual, making Tatiana feel warmly embraced.

"I know, I'm sorry," Tatiana admits, "I was hoping we could go swimming tonight?"

—

Having made the evening plans, she sits down to face her stubborn canvas once more. The perspective of cutting through the cold swimming pool water slowly relaxes her nerves, knowing that relief will come soon.

She picks up her brush, feeling ready to advance the painting. Thin webs of sketches lay covered by paint, here and there still showing their little dark veins. Tatiana came to like the river she created, its stormy water has a delicate quality to it, almost feminine. *A woman whose thoughts seem to storm,* she sings to herself, thinking over the next strokes of paint. Little spirits of abandoned clothes soon populate the wind-dragged grass, stretching out their sleeves and legs. Proud of the flow of her work, Tatiana notices an unusual-for-her softness in all this, her brush blurs the harsh borders of color, giving the painting a new, impressionistic quality. She sits back, perplexed, and a new thought begins to creep around her mind. Shadows of premonition tingle her eyes, recognizing Ellie's style. Scornful, she gets away from the painting, having to begin preparing for her outing either way.

She looks around her disheveled bedroom for the swimsuit she stashed away somewhere a long time ago, coming back from some trip or other. The old love for swimming begins flowing through her veins anew, excitement lightening her step. She hasn't gone out to swim with Marcel in what seems like ages, since both their careers began picking up pace.

The doorbell rings, just as she manages to dig the swimsuit out from underneath her bed.

—

"Like the old days," says Marcel, showing Tatiana to his car.

He came to pick her up to celebrate the tradition, even though these days Tatiana owns a car. She smiles, proud of how far they both managed to come.

"Like the old days," she repeats, getting inside.

The way to their favorite pool is only around ten minutes by car, but the road is made torturous by constant renovations, turning it into a never-ending building site. Dust and sand stick to wheels, and the traffic moves astonishingly slow.

"What a joke," sighs Tatiana.

"You never were a very patient person." Marcel shakes his head. "By the way, what prompted the call?"

"Well, first because I really missed you," Tatiana hangs her voice on the prolonged last syllable, stretching it out to make Marcel laugh.

"Yeah, sure. And for real?" He looks to her for a moment, turning away from the road. "Missed you too, by the way. We should've met up sooner."

"Cute," she grins. "No, but you're right. There was a reason; I feel very confused as of late. I need a good swim," she admits.

Marcel nods, knowing the curing potential of immersing oneself wholly in water. There is a mind-soothing quality to swimming, an almost purifying component that he often benefits from as a transgressive artist. His great influence is the art of Robert Mapplethorpe, and the heavy subject manner makes him seek out comfort frequently.

"It's kind of like a womb, no?" He thinks out loud, making Tatiana giggle.

"Maybe. But wombs are cozy and warm. The swimming pool is freezing. Uninviting. Maybe it's the freshness that makes your blood flow differently through your brain?"

The debate rolls until they arrive at the pool, with no clear winner.

"I guess it depends on your mood," Marcel concludes. "Bathtubs are definitely little wombs."

"Yes," Tatiana nods as they enter.

The strong smell of chlorine hits their noses as soon as they shut the door. Tatiana is overcome by a wave of nostalgia, looking at the kids running around the corridor, half in swimsuits, half-clothed, shouting carelessly to each other. There is such a distinct atmosphere in these spaces that she feels a strong urge to translate it into painting, regretting leaving her sketchbook behind.

"Marcel," she turns to her friend, "do you have your phone on you?"

"Always," he smiles, taking out his phone. "Why?"

"I'd like for you to take some pictures to capture the swimming pool vibe." She gestures towards the floor tiles, the half-empty vending machines, flip flops on the floor. "I think I want to paint it."

"That's hardly a landscape," he says with a smile, "but the pictures would be really nice. You got it." He tells her, snapping a few pics before turning to go inside the men's changing room.

Tatiana follows suit and enters the women's locker room, considering how everything makes her feel. The shared nudity of changing rooms has fascinated her ever since entering it for the first time. Truth be told, it was her first opportunity to study anatomy as a girl, her stares sometimes verging on rude. Her mother had to unglue her eyes from various breasts and legs, young and old, a sea of diverse hair tucked into swimming caps. The swimming pool escapades drove her towards painting women, on the way discovering her budding sexuality. Eventually, she abandoned the subject, but her deep appreciation for the female body stayed with her. Now, knowing better than to treat the swimmers as her anatomy subjects, she admires the simple utilitarianism of the changing room space; bright yellow lockers keep her keys contained in their metallic stomachs, now and then clinking in response to some accidental elbow or knee strike. Girls in swimsuits of various shades of pink run around, impatient for their mothers to emerge out of the room. Tatiana finishes changing and heads towards the showers, always dysregulated, spitting out either steaming water straight from the pits of Hell or ice cold, marking her entire skin with goosebumps. One time she overheard some teenagers joke, *"It's just like my ex!"* pointing at the shower, and Tatiana hasn't been able to forget that line ever since.

Feeling her thoughts thoroughly granulated by the moody stream, she steps out into the swimming area. Having forgotten to take her flip flops, her toenails curl not to slip on the watered floor. She waves to the already-swimming Marcel, but he fails to see, prompting her to simply enter the pool. She used to properly warm up before swimming, but now has no more patience to do that, craving to simply flow amidst the refreshing water, alongside the other swimmers. Solitary, but still having others within reach, she feels free.

They swim until the late-night hour empties the hall, and impatient staff have to remind them that the pool closes in fifteen minutes.

Tatiana comes out of the water, shivering, at peace. Marcel gets their towels hanging from the wall, and they head towards their respective changing rooms.

"See you in the lobby." He waves to Tatiana, and she nods in response.

Changing back into her clothes has always been the worst part of swimming, she ruefully remembers. The still-wet limbs infect her clothes with water in a particularly unpleasant manner, making each sleeve sticky and stubbornly difficult to put on. The room is now completely empty, putting her in an uneasy mood. The space feels like something liminal, an Edward Hopper scene with a solitary woman, sitting in front of a row of yellow metal lockers, drying her hair with an already wet towel. Wanting to quickly escape this unsettling solitude, she hurriedly packs everything into her bag and leaves to reunite with Marcel.

She finds him chatting with the receptionist, probably to mitigate the annoyance they caused by staying until the last minute. Fortunately, Marcel is a naturally charming man, so they manage to avoid any unpleasantness.

Once out of the building, neither of them wants to go home.

"The night feels so fresh," Marcel sighs into the peaceful air of the quiet neighborhood.

Tatiana's stomach rumbles unforgivingly, causing them both to laugh.

"I'm starving," she exclaims, feeling the hunger permeating her muscles.

"Let's get hot dogs," Marcel suggests. "Remember the hot dog truck, not so far from here? I bet it's still there."

And they go, feeling like two silly adolescents hunting for food trucks. Tatiana feels the air fill her lungs to the brim with life, her tired muscles ache, reminding her that her body is in its prime, lively, present. She hasn't felt so at peace with herself for a long while.

"Hey, Marcel," she says.

"Hm?" he responds, seemingly going through a similar state of bliss.

"I have girl problems." Tatiana grins, ready to be open about her troubles.

"No way," Marcel laughs, though he can sense that she is serious. "More like woman problems now, I guess."

"More like woman problems," she sighs.

They get to the truck, indeed still serving the same hot dogs they used to get two years ago. The rich smell of meat and ketchup sends their stomachs rumbling insanely. Tatiana gets her usual, with pickles and mustard, and they sit on the curb, simply eating and enjoying having each other around. When Marcel swallows his last bite, he wipes his hands and clears his throat, ready to give his best advice.

"So, who's the woman?" he asks.

"I'm afraid you know her," Tatiana admits. "It's the painter, Ellie Matthews."

Even saying the name out loud sends shivers down her spine, her unruly thoughts sent spiraling back towards the infamous bathroom stall.

"Oh." Marcel thinks it over. "But it makes sense, no? You even paint similar things. And she's hot. Like ethereal goddess hot."

"But it's so much more than that. I don't like her approach to art. I don't like her style. We argued horribly the first time we met, and then hooked up during her exhibition opening," Tatiana finally spits out the string of events plaguing her mind.

He exhales loudly, taking in all the unexpected information.

"You... hooked up during her vernissage?" He laughs a bit.

"Yes, but you don't get it. She has such a calm demeanor, when we're not arguing at least, her art is so delicate, but then—" Tatiana blushes, only slightly, "She's insane at sex."

Marcel laughs, heartily.

"So what do you feel like you want to do? Why not just forget about the whole affair, if it upsets you so much you need to go swimming? Or you just want more of the insane sex? Because that is ok, you know?"

Tatiana pouts her lips. She doesn't know.

"There's something that stirs me in her, like I haven't been this mad about art for a long time. And then... I'm painting this thing now, and it's so pathetically, clearly influenced by her."

Marcel pats her back, shaking his head.

"Girl, you're down so bad!"

"No, stop it." She waves her hand around.

They finally get up and stroll towards the car, regretful to not be able to walk home on foot.

"Someday, someday they'll finish this bloody road," Marcel chants as they climb up the hill towards the parking lot.

"Someday they will," Tatiana nods, grateful to have friends who get aggravated at road construction because of the desire to walk under the stars.

Tired, they don't speak much on their way back, listening to whatever the radio host chooses to play.

And I do want more of the insane sex.

I can still feel her inside me and I like it.

8

ELLIE

Ellie stares at the waterfall, mad to have decided to continue it either way. The bubbling water springs down, cascading into the lake below. The hills bend over the phenomenon in a manner she finds mocking. As if the hills were bent over her, looking straight into the pits of her artistic soul, looking for substance. She feels empty, bendable like a straw of grass exposed to barely any wind. How come it takes so little for her delicate touch to turn into something violent?

She wipes her hands clean and decides to order dinner in. Afternoon has turned to evening, and she can see the windows of nearby apartments light up. She has always liked to spy on people through their windows, observing their kitchens or living rooms—the scenes of their rituals. Little figures dancing around, preparing dinner or taking their shoes off, coming home from work. As a student, she painted a project meant to imagine her as a little figure stared at from someone else's perspective. Back then she lived in a little, square studio apartment, and the series of four paintings included the four corners of her room; Ellie cooking soup on her little portable gas stove, Ellie reading a book on her miniature bed, Ellie putting on her socks next to the pile of clothing substituting a wardrobe, and Ellie at her canvas, despairing over some project.

She smiles, thinking it over, a little upset that she has no idea where the paintings went. The delivery man rings the doorbell with urgency, stirring her out of the river of thoughts.

"Thank you, have a good evening," she says at the door, impatient to eat.

The clouds of steam from the noodles explode in her face, the carton box almost burning her hands. She sits down on the floor, far away from any painting, afraid to grease or stain something of value. The thick strings of noodles slide around her mouth, delicious.

Suddenly, her phone rings. She curses herself for the lack of napkins, having already used the ones provided, and grabs the phone awkwardly, knowing that an unknown number could mean something particularly important.

"Yes?" she utters, right after swallowing.

"Is this Ellie Matthews?" a low-pitched, male voice inquires.

"Yes, speaking."

"This is George Kirsch calling, from the Kirsch Gallery of Art, I had the honor to see your recent exhibition, and decided to reach out with an, I hope, interesting offer."

Ellie sits completely still. She knows the Kirsch Gallery, now managed and curated by Samuel Kirsch's son, George.

"Of course, I'm listening," she assures, intrigued.

"I want to suggest to you a collaborative project that my gallery would host with pleasure," he continues, "I propose a meeting tomorrow, if your availability would allow?"

Having settled the hour, they hang up. Ellie looks at the cooled down noodles with disbelief, giddy from excitement. She hopes that a new project will give her some new sense of direction, besides the obvious growth of her recognition. She paces around the studio, impatient for the following days, the mist of late evening darkness seeps into the room, prompting her to leave for home.

—

Next morning, she doesn't hesitate for even a second to firmly step out of the bed. The meeting is supposed to take place at 11am, and she cannot even think of being late, a worry she likes to exaggerate, for she rarely ever is late, even a few minutes. The weather outside seems fresh and encouraging, finally allowing her to wear a dress. Paired with a vintage blazer, she looks feminine but powerfully professional. Her heavy gold jewelry ornaments her ears and neck, but her fingers are left free and agile. She's not in the mood for rings.

For breakfast, she prepares only a light sandwich with cottage cheese and tomatoes, feeling too nervous to eat anything too heavy. Little crystals of salt catch the morning light beautifully, sparkling in her eyes.

On the way, she listens to some upbeat jazz

music from a spring playlist she undug from piles of others for this occasion. The road is jammed per usual, but she truly has pools of time ahead of her, the clock displaying the blissful hour, 10:20.

—

She pushes the office door open and freezes in a trembling surprise.

"Good morning, Ms Matthews," Kirsch says, inviting her to sit.

Opposite him sits Tatiana Khan. Hearing the surname, Tatiana hurriedly turns around, her shimmering copper red braid splendidly flowing with the motion.

"Hi, Ellie," she says, seemingly surprised as well. "How are you doing?"

Ellie sits down, uncertain, remembering Tatiana crying out Ellie's name as she came.

"Hi, Tatiana," she says at last. She remains cool on the surface.

George Kirsch nods, content, apparently not expecting the two to know each other.

"Ah, I see that you two have already been introduced. Splendid," he says, before taking a sip from his cup. "The gallery has been observing the work

of both of you. We, I especially, consider the two of
you visionary artists of our age. Many pointed out
the similarities and the seeming sync in which
your art flows, which prompted me to offer an
exhibition combining your art. You would work
together on whatever theme you'd like, the only
condition being that you create it together. I can
see such a collaboration attracting much attention." He smiles, proud of the idea. "What would
you say? How much time do you need to think?"
he asks, looking from one to another.

*No. Absolutely not. I'm not working with her. I
hate her.*

Ellie stirs on her seat. She was not expecting
any of this to go the way it is going, but even
though her emotions resemble a thunderstorm,
her mind seems clear on the subject. Such an
opportunity is certainly to be taken, no matter her
personal feelings regarding Tatiana Khan. She
swore to make her career as grand as possible, and
she wasn't going to step down now. She turns to
regard Tatiana's reaction.

Tatiana is knitting her brows together, a habit
Ellie noted as frequent on her striking face. Her
wide set brown eyes are enchanting. Ellie can't
help but note.

"I'm not so sure, our processes of creation seem to be very different..." she says carefully.

Ellie's face heats up, determined not to lose the opportunity.

"Tatiana, we can make this work. I'm certain of it," she says, as calmly as possible, not to seem desperate. Ellie knew she needed to take control of this. It was an excellent opportunity for both of them.

George Kirsch looks at his watch and back up at the artists.

"I suggest you talk it through and get back to me once you reach a consensus." He looks at Ellie, "Counting on you, Ms Matthews."

Getting out of the office, Ellie is upset to be reduced to the desperate one, having to convince Tatiana to participate. She would prefer to complete the project on her own, but the choice isn't theirs, and she's used to building with what she's got.

Nearing the exit of the gallery, Tatiana unexpectedly turns to Ellie.

"To put it simply, because I want to be honest with you," Tatiana begins, "the prospect of working with you makes me nervous. You seem to hold very different opinions, and you have made your distaste for my art clear, and that would not put me in the right mindset to express myself." She exhales, visibly having thought these words through before.

Ellie stops, quite charmed by her openness.

"I get it. I understand," she responds. Looking into Tatiana's dark brown eyes makes her remember their hot and dirty fucking, causing something between her legs to stir. "But this is a huge opportunity for both of us. I'm sure we can find a way to collaborate, we can even agree on the vision and work entirely separately. But I need this, really. Tatiana, I do," she finishes.

Like you needed my hand inside of you.

"Let's get lunch," Tatiana suggests and Ellie admires the sway of the younger woman's hips. Tatiana is hot, all seductive curves and flame red messy hair and full sensual lips and Ellie hadn't allowed herself to openly think that before.

I allowed myself to fuck her, though. Didn't I?

Ellie agrees, and they head towards the disgustingly business-filled area of the city. Nothing green soothes their eyes, every inch of the ground is bathed by concrete. The sky stands shadowed by the overwhelming skyscrapers, and the sandwich or poke bowl shops seem completely soulless.

"Let's go to the older area?" Ellie offers.

They make their way, inhaling the springtime lightness of air, heading towards the little bustling area nearby. Once there, they're welcomed by the delicious scents of freshly cooked food, steam flowing out of the tiny, crowded kitchens.

"What are you in the mood for?" Tatiana asks, spreading her arms wide.

She smiles generously, and Ellie knows that it's partially because she has the upper hand in the conversation. *A foolish little play*, she thinks, considering what her squeezed-by-stress stomach would like.

"Dumplings?" she suggests, pointing to a Chinese stand with some three or four chairs in front.

"Let's go," agrees Tatiana, light-footed and seemingly excited.

They sit down, holding their orders' little printed numbers. Tatiana's number is seven.

"Look, mine is lucky," she says with a grin.

Ellie has no idea why Tatiana seems to over-flow with joy. Her every move seems to possess some secret to happiness, entirely perplexing, she thinks, her own smile going unnoticed.

"I have never heard of seven being lucky," she says as she shakes her head. Her family wasn't particularly superstitious, failing to pass on many such common concepts.

"At least in Russia, it's very lucky." Tatiana shrugs.

And there it is, her order comes out of the kitchen first. Ellie looks down on her "unlucky" number six, still in the belly of the loud and hot kitchen.

"Does that mean," she begins, the scent of dumplings finally awakening her hunger, "I unluckily will lose the exhibition?" She looks up from the plate, to face Tatiana.

Tatiana doesn't wait, but packs her mouth full of chicken dumplings, chewing blissfully. She puts one finger in the air, telling Ellie to wait. In the meantime, they hear a cook shout, "*Number six!*" and Ellie gets up to get her food.

When she's back, Tatiana's plate lies half-empty.

"No, Ellie. Maybe it's good to do something uncomfortable," she admits, picking up another dumpling. "I'll do the exhibition with you."

Tatiana smiles, and her sensual lips glisten in the warm sun. Ellie cannot keep her eyes away, as if a star pulled towards another by the enduring strength of gravity. She craves to feel these lips against hers once more, remembering all too vividly the sensations of that evening. Giving in to the rush of relief, Ellie bends over the little wooden table and clashes her lips with Tatiana's.

When she pulls away, both women look at each other with feelings mixed across their faces.

"I don't know…" begins Tatiana, but soon the words she meant to say seem to get stuck in her throat.

Ellie's heart beats incessantly fast when she realizes how easily she caved in to the feeling. "I'm sorry, if you didn't want to—" she begins saying, but doesn't finish, finding her lips licked by Tatiana's tongue, invitingly.

"Okay, we shouldn't do this here, though, this is obscene," she laughs, relieved.

They finish their lunch in peace, having resolved at least some aspects of their troubles. Ellie feels a wave of joy, thinking about working on the project. She suspiciously notices that the joy seems to come from the perspective of working with Tatiana as well, but she keeps that feeling to herself.

"So... Do we kiss, now, casually?" she asks Tatiana, wanting some form of clarification.

"Apparently," the other laughs it off, clearly shying away from some conversation.

Ellie decides to let it go for the moment.

"Should we call Kirsch?" she asks, hoping to settle the matter entirely.

"Go ahead," Tatiana says, wiping her lips clean. "I have to keep going." She gets up. "Do you even have my number?" She smiles.

"I... Well, if it's the same one—"

"No, it's not the same one as the one that'll take you to my manager," she laughs, picking up the napkin and scribbling on it. "There you go, see you later!" She waves goodbye and is gone, soaked into the crowd.

Ellie sits for a while, looking at her two leftover dumplings and the slightly greased napkin with Tatiana's number on it.

She sighs and picks up her phone to call the curator.

9

TATIANA

Tatiana feels her phone vibrate, just as she's pouring wine into her friend's glass. She sits back down to check the message, surrounded by the lively chatter of her companions.

Tomorrow 10 at my studio? – Ellie.

Tatiana adds the number to her contact list, before responding, *Am or Pm?*

She puts the phone back, listening in to something Connie began saying. The phone vibrates again.

Am, very funny. The address is Pearl St, 284.

Tatiana turns the word *Pearl* over in her mind, delighting in its sound. What a good omen, she thinks, finally able to enjoy the conversation.

"So as I was saying," Connie excitedly exclaims, to the numerous hushes reminding her of them being in a restaurant, "All love is just desire wearing fancy clothes."

Tatiana watches everyone's reaction, thinking the proposition over.

"No, I don't think that's true," Tatiana says. "Sometimes it starts out this way, sure. But you can't tell me that the old couples we see strolling down the park alleys, picking out flowers for each other despite their hurting backs, are in love based solely on desire?"

"No, but if it started out that way, isn't it its core?" Connie asks, pouring herself more of the ruby red wine.

"No, maybe the core fluctuates?" responds Tatiana, spinning the slippery spaghetti around her fork.

"No, I think it's just that. Sex. Sometimes you fall for the most unexpected person, why? Because you want their dick," she concludes, making the table laugh wildly. Tatiana smiles, compassionate. Everyone knew Connie's affair with Terry was a matter of weeks, besides Connie herself, apparently.

"I just feel so old. Like, I'm thirty next week,

and I still keep running around in circles," she sighs.

The table quiets down, everyone relating the sentiment to themselves, measuring the degree to which their own lives correspond. Marcel, invited last minute by Tatiana, almost hid his engagement ring under his plate.

"Alright, thanks for the reminder, Connie," Tatiana jokes, trying to lighten up the mood.

Truth be told, she began noticing these thoughts float around her own mind, feeling that her unstable dating is unbecoming for her age. Remembering her parents' family life at 28, she often sinks in embarrassment. On the other hand, hers is a different generation, with its own customs.

"Let's all get dessert," Marcel suggests.

–

Back in her bedroom, undressing to shower, Tatiana remembers her appointment with Ellie. She sets up an avalanche of alarms to be released in the morning, praying to whatever has the power to let her be on time. Her recently deepening habit of sleeping in began getting on her nerves, very un-springlike. She gets in the shower, and the water drops hit her back in a pleasant massage, relaxing the tense muscles. She sings little fragments of songs to herself, content with her place in life, even though quite unsettled romantically.

—

The violence of alarms hitting her ears makes her regret every choice she has made up until this point. She tries shielding herself from the flood of sounds, but to no avail. Looking at the time, she understands she needs to hurry up. Reluctantly, she gets on her feet, sleepy and disturbed.

"This is no state to create," she mutters under her breath, picking out underwear from her overflowing drawer.

She grabs an apple and a pre-bought cappuccino from her fridge, checking the way to Ellie's studio. Tatiana is decidedly not a morning person, which she always thought only added to her artistic personality. Perhaps she was wrong.

The stream of words running out of the radio makes her dizzy so she turns it off, welcoming the quiet. In silence, she drives towards Pearl Street, already lamenting the lack of spaces to park. She decides to call Ellie.

"Hey," she decides to get straight to the point, "where can I leave my car?"

After finding out that Ellie's studio comes with a parking lot, Tatiana is in a much better mood. Ascending the stairs, she's not even mad about the lack of an elevator.

–

"Hi," Ellie welcomes her, opening the door. "You're almost on time!" she mocks. She is smug and perfect.

"What do you mean, I am on time."

"It's 10 past 10, but that's perfectly fine," Ellie says, letting Tatiana pass through.

"I supplied the studio with another chair," she adds, showing the way.

Tatiana stands for a moment, taking the space in. It's a simple, wall-less space, entirely committed to letting in as much light as possible. The gigantic windows flood the room with light, the space remains uncluttered—she can find only a simple desk, a pair of easels, and a cabinet for supplies.

"You're insane," Tatiana concludes. "How do you even keep this space so clean?"

Ellie smiles proudly, holding tidiness as an important value.

"To be fair, it is quite new. But I like to keep things neat," she admits.

Tatiana shakes her head, approaching the desk. There are some sketches lying around and printed pictures of the gallery room they'll have available for the project. She sits down, taking some in her hands.

"Have you already started thinking it over?" she asks, slightly annoyed at herself for not doing the same.

"Yes, you can see all the sketches I made. I think it would be nice to incorporate the space into the process, since we're in the unique position of knowing where we'll exhibit."

Tatiana nods.

"So, what do you think of painting the same spaces, but each of us in our own style, then exhibiting them back to back?" she suggests.

"That's a bit banal, don't you think?" Ellie stops and glances at Tatiana, "I'm sorry, that was unnecessary. I just think maybe we should do something more original."

Tatiana shrugs, not particularly attached to the idea either way. In truth, she's not good at conceptualizing her art, she usually allows herself to go with the flow of her creation, not predicting or planning anything.

"Listen, I'm not good at this," she says. "I usually go with my impulses."

"That's okay," Ellie smiles. "I do the same. I rarely plan my work."

They sit still, not sure how to conceptualize a collaborative project this way and still give it their unique essence.

"How about we blend our work in a unique way," Tatiana suggests, "by painting the other's sketch?"

Ellie sits back, pondering. She keeps playing with the rings on her fingers, twisting and turning them around. Tatiana sits transfixed by them, the seemingly measured and controlled intervals with which Ellie touches each ring.

"It is a pretty simple idea," she admits, "but I think it can grow into something interesting."

"We shouldn't paint landscapes," fires Tatiana, suddenly certain of the course their work should take. "That's too obvious and we choose similar subjects anyway," she adds.

"Oh, that's interesting," Ellie puts her head in her hands, ready to listen.

"I have some barely started or barely conceptualized work, I'm sure you do, too," Tatiana continues. "We can make an exchange and thus fuse the art into something completely new."

Ellie seems to consent to the idea. Tatiana feels relieved, wanting to work on the paintings already, instead of spending hours on debating the concept. She feels her best when actually painting.

"Should we meet another time then, with the sketches ready?" Ellie asks, looking around her studio. "I don't know if I have a lot of suitable ideas. The last one..." She pauses.

"The last one?" Tatiana prompts, surprised by the sudden pause.

"I grew kind of angry with it, because of you, to be honest."

"Because of me?" Tatiana laughs. "How so?"

Ellie goes to the easel holding her waterfall painting, turning it around to show Tatiana.

"It's not my style. It feels aggressive and influenced by you," she says, almost accusatory.

Tatiana gets closer to the roughly begun painting. Its vibrance indeed seems to resemble hers, but she feels slightly offended by the suggestion that her art is merely *aggressive*.

"Is that what you think about my art, Ellie?" Tatiana turns to look at her. "Solely *aggressive*, solely *bold*, maybe?"

Ellie sits down, tilting her chin towards the ceiling in an act of resignation.

"No, Tatiana, no, that's not what I think. Why can't we let this silly bickering go?" She returns to looking back at Tatiana. The abundant light colors her eyes particularly bright, making them gleam pleasantly from Tatiana's face. Ellie smiles delicately.

"You look very pretty in this light," she says. "Blooming."

"Oh," Tatiana blushes. She can't believe how easily Ellie can get her to do that. "I'm still offended at how angry you are to resemble my style," she add as she shakes fluttering thoughts away, still standing by the canvas. "I mean, the painting is nice."

"Nice?" Ellie scoffs. "It's nothing, and I don't want it anymore. It looks like every brush stroke was made with strain, heavy, full of effort."

Tatiana shakes her head. "I disagree," she says.

"Ah, stop it." Ellie gets flustered.

She gets up from the chair and joins Tatiana in inspecting the painting, hopeful to gain some new perspective that would save it in her eyes. Getting close, Tatiana's scent swirls around her nose. She stands only inches away from Tatiana's neck, seeing all the little unruly strands of red hair escape her band tied tightly around it, an endearing detail available only to those close enough. The strong, woody perfume overshadows the natural scent of Tatiana's skin, but not entirely. Craving to feel the warmth of her skin against herself, Ellie stands even closer.

"What are you doing?" Tatiana asks, in a slightly teasing tone.

"Getting closer to you."

The naked sentence pleasantly shocks Tatiana's ears.

"Why?" she asks, turning around to find herself face to face with Ellie, separated by barely any distance at all. The tips of their noses almost kiss.

"Because I smelled your perfume," Ellie licks Tatiana's bottom lip gently, then continues, "and I felt I needed to feel more of you." She gets back at licking, tracing along Tatiana's lips.

Tatiana feels like she might combust there and

then on the spot. She feels a familiar excitement buzzing between her legs.

"Oh yeah?" Tatiana's hands run along Ellie's thighs, all the way up to her ass, circling.

Ellie lets out a quiet sigh, almost into Tatiana's ear. Hearing Ellie moan gets her off more than she imagined. She grabs her ass tighter.

"Yes," Ellie nods, mischievous.

"Feel me then." Tatiana's hands find the pants' zipper and pull it down. She slides the pants to the ground and spreads Ellie's legs a bit further apart.

"What are you doing?" Ellie whispers, curious and thirsty for touch.

Tatiana slaps her ass lightly.

"Be patient," she shakes her head. "I didn't get much of you last time. I want to, now."

She gets down on her knees in front of Ellie, pulling her pussy towards her face by holding her ass tightly. With Ellie's underwear still on, she starts slowly licking it up and down her lips, feeling the material get moist on both sides. She puts more pressure, burying her face in between Ellie's thighs.

"Spread them wider for me," she asks. Ellie follows suit.

"Oh, you like being told what to do?" Tatiana grins into Ellie's wet pussy.

Ellie shakes her head.

"When you do it, I feel such a mixture of feelings it really turns me on." She runs her fingers through Tatiana's hair. "It's like my mind has no idea what to do, so my body takes over and gets horny."

"I like that," Tatiana chuckles. "I want to eat you out on the table."

She gets up from her knees, giving Ellie's ass another slap of encouragement.

They get to the table, and she pushes the drawings aside as Ellie lays down. Tatiana removes Ellie's underwear finally and begins working with her tongue, circling and sliding. Ellie tightens her grip on Tatiana's hair.

Her legs begin dancing around Tatiana's head, thighs pulsing with the sweetest rhythm. Tatiana speeds up, ever so slightly, feeling how wet Ellie's gotten right in her mouth.

She lifts her head up.

"You're so wet for me, honey"

"Just fuck me, please," Ellie utters, horribly taken out of the rhythm.

Tatiana climbs on the table, laying right atop Ellie.

"I'll fuck you to death, and I want to see you die right next to my face," she says, kissing Ellie's lips. "Can you taste yourself?"

"Mhm," Ellie nods.

"Good," Tatiana says, reaching in between Ellie's legs.

Ellie spreads them out greedily, begging to be touched. Tatiana begins tracing them with her hand, without any rush, with a feather-like gentleness. Sometimes she gets almost close enough, but then her fingers make another detour, torturing, infuriating.

"Please, fuck me," Ellie moans, wet and spread out on the table.

"Should I?" Tatiana teases, fingers rolling around on the delicate skin.

"Yes," Ellie nods, desperate.

Tatiana's fingers finally seem on the right track, sliding around and finally, she lets one finger into Ellie.

"Are you sure?"

"Yes, please."

She slides in the second one, moving only

slightly, still only teasing, looking deep into Ellie's hungry eyes.

"Do you want to get fucked, Ellie?"

"Yes, I'm begging you," she moans.

Having heard what she wanted, Tatiana gets to work. Her agile fingers know their way around Ellie's body surprisingly well, stretching her out and pressing with a steady rhythm. Ellie's voice sounds particularly pretty when moaning, Tatiana thinks, looking at the hardened nipples through Ellie's shirt.

"Take the shirt off for me," she instructs, as her fingers continue to fuck Ellie.

Ellie struggles but follows through, exposing herself obediently. Tatiana gets closer and starts licking Ellie's nipples while fucking her, feeling for her G spot, tongue tracing little circles on her nipples, her thumb against Ellie's clitoris.

When Ellie's thighs begin shivering, she knows she's close. Her head bends back, and she cries out loudly as she squirts filling the palm of Tatiana's hand.

Tatiana smiles to herself as Ellie Matthews, the ethereal goddess comes apart for her fingers.

—

Laying together on the table, the two cuddle, watching the street stretching outside the gigantic window. Their legs lay intertwined, Tatiana's head next to Ellie's chest. Their breathing flows steady and deep, unified.

"Well, it's nice we can lie here this time," says Tatiana after a while of silence.

"True," Ellie admits. "I was feeling kind of bad to leave you on the cubicle floor last time we fucked.."

"Yeah, I was feeling kind of angry about that, I think, but I just pushed the feeling away," Tatiana says. "It's a vulnerable thing."

They hold each other closer, each thinking her own thing. Tatiana's back begins hurting from lying on the unforgiving surface, but she tries to ignore the discomfort. There is something infinitely calming for her in Ellie's arms, something she doesn't usually get from hook ups.

"I like your studio," she says.

"I like it too." Ellie smiles. "It's exactly the way I imagined when I started art school."

They fall back into the soft embrace of silence, but it doesn't feel unnatural. Their silence feels right, filling in the space between them like a pillow. Looking at the time, Tatiana realizes she soon has to go.

"Ellie, it's 1pm already!" She disentangles her limbs, looking for a graceful way to slide down from the table. "I have lunch scheduled with someone for 2:30, and I still need to change," she says, more to clarify the plan to herself rather than inform Ellie about the details.

"You still have time." Ellie gets up too, only now beginning to feel the consequences of lying so long on the table. She puts her pants back on, struggling to zip them back.

"Tatiana, you broke my zipper!"

Tatiana looks up, in the middle of tying her shoes. She grins.

"Sorry!"

They both laugh, suddenly realizing the absurdity of their relationship. Each feels a little bit younger when around the other, and their sex brings much refreshment to both of their lives. Tatiana gets up from the floor, her shoelaces tied, her bag hanging from her shoulder.

They share a brisk kiss, a quick goodbye, and she's on her way. Her steps remain light, and the perspective of working with Ellie is no longer a daunting one.

10

ELLIE

The doorbell rings so loudly and suddenly that Ellie drops her cup to the floor, shattering it into a sea of sharp glass specks.

"A moment!" she shouts, irritated.

She knows it's Fred, which means the door can wait. The remains of the cup now richly decorate the floor, hundreds of hazardous little tears. The late spring sun shines through them, here and there painting a rainbow on the bright floor. Ellie takes the broom and begins cleaning up, Fred still waiting outside.

"What the hell took you so long?" he explodes when she finally opens the door.

"It's your fault, you shattered my favorite cup,"

she points to the gathered glass, sitting on the dustpan.

They embrace and she sets the water to boil for some tea, impatient to show him the paintings stashed all around her room.

"Why there and not the studio?" Fred inquires.

"You know, I like to keep these ones close, I don't fully know why." Ellie smiles. "I think we're doing lots of good work, Tatiana and I."

"I'm sure," smiles Fred, "the whole thing still astonishes me."

"Me too," Ellie sighs, a thought or two passing through her mind before she pours the water.

They take their cups and walk towards the bedroom. The hallway is not very well lit, as opposed to the rest of the flat, giving it a rather tunnel-like feeling. Once they reach the bedroom, they're welcomed back by sweeping light.

"You know, I don't think I have ever even seen your bedroom," Fred wonders, looking for the paintings.

"Yeah, I don't usually have men in here," Ellie retorts while opening the door to her wardrobe.

"No! Don't tell me you stashed them in your wardrobe, Ellie."

She turns to him, surprised.

"Why not? It's a spacious room," she says, taking them out one by one. "And you know how much I hate cluttered space."

Fred shakes his head in disbelief, but soon his attention is caught on the spiky fence of Ellie's work. He gets closer to one painting, inspecting it with deep interest.

It portrays a swimming pool scene, women getting dressed before going out to swim. The background is yellow, something uncommon in Ellie's work, even though the piece preserves her somber touch. He can almost feel the chlorine fill up his nose, overcome by childhood memories.

"Wow," he says. "What the hell prompted you to choose this subject?"

"That's the whole point," Ellie explains. "Didn't I tell you? We took each other's sketches, so I'm painting Tatiana's ideas, and she's painting mine. The vision is simple, but I think it is effective, right? I like the challenge of respecting the sketch while preserving my own voice."

Fred looks to another painting, seemingly more abstract. Groups of entangled materials gallop through the canvas, endearingly lively.

"So you're working with no theme?"

"There is a theme, it's subversion of each

other's abilities," Ellie sits down on her bed, sipping the tea. "We often work together in the studio, sometimes interfering, sometimes flowing with each other. It's exhilarating."

"Alright, I see."

Fred sits down next to her.

"And how is your relationship going? Last time we spoke you weren't that happy about it."

Ellie takes another sip, embarrassed that she forgot their recent phone call. She bites her lip, conflicted whether she wants to confide in Fred. He can be indelicate, to put it lightly, often preferring to plunge straight into giving advice instead of simply listening. Perhaps she could use some advice at the moment, Ellie thinks, turning to Fred.

"Okay, so we still haven't talked about it."

"What do you mean? Like at all? You didn't acknowledge that you're fucking?"

Ellie looks away, confronted by the harshness of the word *fucking* thrown at her.

"We did acknowledge that," she considers whether *acknowledged* is truly the right word for what they did, "but nothing...more? It's strange, it's like she's completely avoiding the subject of what we are."

"And what would that be?" Fred asks, straight-forward.

Ellie feels something tighten around her chest. She's mad at Tatiana for being so elusive, but she feels that the lack of conversation also protects her own feelings, even though often craving clarity.

"I don't know. We sleep with each other, spend time together, kiss, and that's kind of it." "Well, sounds like you're a couple to me," Fred announces.

Ellie again feels her chest, but now her stomach joins in too. She has not allowed herself to think about them in these terms, fearing that for Tatiana all this was much less serious.

"I don't think she's that serious about it," she sighs.

"But you are?"

"Not if she isn't."

Fred erupts with laughter, spilling some of the tea on his shirt.

"Ellie, for Christ's sake, you're almost 40! This sounds like high school all over again. Just take her out, be upfront about your feelings, and ask about hers. It's that simple and that difficult."

Ellie nods, feeling slightly childish herself.

There isn't much more to say, she only needs to face the reality of possible rejection.

"What if she's not serious about this, and we have to keep working together?"

"Well then," Fred says, getting up, "You'll just finish it off somehow. From what I can see you're kind of ahead. Look, I need to get going."

He lost his bag somewhere, now looking all over Ellie's room.

"Fred, the bag is in the kitchen," she reminds him. Her memory has always been the best.

Saying her goodbyes at the doorstep, Ellie feels somewhat confident in what steps she should take, grateful for allowing Fred to express his opinion.

"Talk to you soon," he says, turning to go. "Really—talk to her," he adds.

"Will do," she smiles and softly closes the door behind him. Once alone, she knows it's time to set up the dreaded date. *I can't even call these dinners dates,* she thinks as she shakes her head.

As if willed by fate, her phone rings.

"Hey Ellie," Tatiana says seemingly out of breath.

"Hey, are you alright?"

"Yes! I've been swimming. I have a question. Do you have teal paint?"

"Yes... What do you need it for?"

"I want to make the house you sketched—you know the one?"

"The Italian one?" Ellie shifts uncomfortably. This was the most difficult sketch to let go of, but Tatiana insisted she could make it beautiful. The house used to belong to Ellie's grandparents, originally coming from Italy. She visited it last summer.

"Yeah, I want to make the palette colder, more blue."

Ellie holds her breath in. She always imagined painting the house in a warm, nostalgic palette. Ideally making its shadows soft, enveloping, sweet.

"But why blue?" she asks, carefully.

"Well... I can tell you about it later, just drop me off the paint sometime?"

Ellie holds onto the phone, nervous.

"Listen, Tatiana, actually—I meant to ask you..."

"Ask me what?" Tatiana's voice conveys a smile, a smile very familiar to Ellie.

"Ask you out to dinner. When are you available?"

"Probably tomorrow evening, if you want?" Tatiana offers.

–

Tomorrow evening came much too soon in Ellie's opinion, leaving her with no time to consider clothes, much less the words she'd like to say. This whole affair muddled her thoughts of herself, always thinking herself very open and clear with relationships. She recognizes that she's a mature woman, reasonably expecting a serious relationship instead of some fling, she keeps reasoning in front of her mirror. Nothing comes together well, so she follows an old piece of advice she once read in some magazine or other: *Difficult conversation? Wear something tried already! Difficult dinners are no time to experiment.*

She settles on her elegant black dress and earrings in the shape of golden drops. She wants to look respectable and decisive but not intimidating. *As if Tatiana would be intimidated.* She laughs. The restaurant they chose, a beautiful place resembling one straight out of Paris, is located conveniently close to her house, only some ten minutes by car.

She sprays on her favorite perfume, citrus and bold, perhaps only slightly too richly, and leaves the apartment. Then needs to go back for her car keys and leave again.

The whole way to the restaurant she's chewing on the words she will have to say, one way or another. She's certain she could get fed on these words alone, their weight fills up her throat and stomach. The traffic jam only worsens her mood; she's now worried about being late as well. Tatiana messages about her own delay, asking whether Ellie will be on time to receive their reserved table.

Of course Ellie will be on time.

—

Finally sitting, Ellie feels like a fool. The elegant restaurant guests sit coupled by dimly lit tables, swift waiters pour expensive wine, glancing at her now and then questioningly. She rolls her eyes apologetically, not knowing what else to do. The delay has spun into fifteen minutes already, and Ellie begins to feel angry.

Tatiana is always late. Always messy. Does Ellie want to be with someone so disorganised?

Finally, the door opens and Tatiana rushes to the table. Her dress catches the delicate sparkling of candles, making her silhouette acquire an almost magical quality. The material wraps her body in elaborate ways, making Ellie's gaze slide around Tatiana's waist, tightly embraced by the fabric. Her necklace sits atop her collarbones with a dignified grace, and looking at Tatiana like this with her shimmering red hair pinned up off her face, Ellie doesn't even remember she was mad.

Tatiana is so beautiful, it is all Ellie can see.

"I'm so sorry, really, I drove through some horrible traffic," Tatiana recites in one breath, "But I'm here, I'm here. I'm really sorry."

Ellie shakes her head. "How is it that you always find a way to be late?" She smiles with forgiveness.

The waiter arrives, seeing that the pair is ready, and gives them the menu cards. Their beige paper discloses everything succinctly. Neither of them being particularly passionate about wine, they choose a recommended white, and take their time to consider the dishes. Ellie feels good being able to practice her calming ritual, a smaller choice made with certainty, leading the bigger choice to seem less overwhelming.

"Alright, I'm considering the asparagus puff pastry," Ellie's eyes jump around the embellished letters, "or the lobster tagliolini."

Tatiana raises her eyebrows, always surprised how much attention Ellie pays these choices.

"I'll take the veal chop," she announces, putting the card to the side.

Ellie looks up from hers, disapprovingly.

"That's awful," she shakes her head.

"What?" Tatiana looks surprised. "What, the meat? The calf?"

Ellie nods.

"Oh, come on, we've talked about this a million times. What about the lobster then?" She laughs, entertained by the sensitive subject.

"I'll take the asparagus then," Ellie says, more as a joke than an actual point.

When the waiter takes their orders, Ellie quiets down. She knows now is the time to begin the conversation. The people around them seem entirely involved in their own problems, loves, or others. Ellie and Tatiana begin looking around, both postponing something.

"Look," Tatiana discreetly points to another couple, "they're about to break up."

The woman is indeed tearing up slightly, having abandoned her Caesar salad completely. The man's head rests in his hands.

"Stop it, give them some privacy," Ellie admonishes her.

"This is a public space, though," Tatiana responds. Then silence follows anew.

Ellie shifts on her seat, knowing that she could easily allow Tatiana to simply carry their conversation away somewhere, far from themselves. *Tonight, this can't happen,* she reminds herself.

"I would like to actually talk to you about something important, and for you to stay on the subject," she begins.

"You sound very condescending," Tatiana informs her, partially correct.

"You're right," Ellie doubles down. "I'm sorry. I do really need to talk, though. Is that okay?"

Tatiana nods.

"I would like..." Ellie clears her throat, "I would like for us to clarify our relationship."

"What does that mean?" Tatiana interrupts. "We do what feels good and stop doing it when it doesn't. That's all I need to know," she concludes, taking a sip of her wine. Her cheeks begin to slowly blush—from wine, candle-warmth, and agitation. Ellie always thought it very endearing, how easily Tatiana can blush.

"Well, I'm glad you're so self-assured," she responds, carefully, "but that's not enough for me. I feel like we're escaping an important conversation. About our feelings."

Their food arrives, steamy and mouth-watering. Ellie can feel her stomach rumble, having eaten only a light breakfast. She's annoyed at the timing but cannot help diving straight into the pastry. Tatiana seems equally hungry, cutting the veal. The conversation endures a break, filled by cutlery and chewing sounds. Ellie from time to time looks up from her plate to Tatiana, feeling more confident already in the middle of the conversation.

They take a break from eating, swirling the surprisingly well-fitted wine around their mouths, heated by the conversation.

"So. What are these feelings?" Tatiana finally lets out, having been holding the question down while eating. The chair suddenly seems much less comfortable.

"Well. That's a question."

They look back down at their plates, at a bit of a loss for words. Ellie decides to be brave and not let herself be intimidated by the situation.

"Look, we're both adults. I like you—" she looks at Tatiana, nervous, her thoughts melting into a little puddle. "I like you a lot, even though we argue often. And I think—" she inhales deeply, "I think I would like us to be together."

Tatiana looks up at her for the first time since Ellie started speaking, her expression quite indiscernible.

"If you don't feel the same way," Ellie continues, "then I suggest we stop seeing each other in this... manner and continue only as friends."

She finishes the sentence and awaits Tatiana's response, her chest tightening and breathing shallow. Regardless of the outcome of the conversation, she's incredibly proud of herself for getting it all out and not allowing herself to drift away from the subject.

Tatiana nods and takes another sip of wine.

"Thank you for saying that," she smiles, "I would like to be with you, too."

She looks down at her hands, visibly thinking of what to say next.

"I think I was afraid that for you it was all just too casual, so I preferred to pretend it was the same for me." She puts her hand across the table, touching Ellie's tenderly.

"I'm glad it was not that," she concludes.

The now-official couple finish their meals, talking at length about the paintings they still need to work on. Ellie remembers about the Italian house, growing slightly less talkative. She doesn't want to damage Tatiana's vision, especially because she gave the sketch away freely, but she also doesn't feel right about letting it go entirely.

"Listen, about the house," she finally begins. "Are you sure you want to make it in a cool palette? It's such a sunny view," she sighs.

"Ellie." Tatiana knits her brows together. "We decided that I can paint it. That means I can do it whatever way I want. There was no indication of a color scheme in the sketch," she softens her statement slightly.

"I know; it's just so personal," Ellie looks away.

"But that's why it's so good," Tatiana says. "You really captured that building. And I know what I'm doing, painting it this way and not another."

Ellie bites her lip. "Can't you keep the tones warm? It's not such a big alteration," she asks, softly. "Just a warm, fuzzy touch of the sun."

Tatiana shakes her head, seemingly feeling uncomfortable.

"Alright, Ellie. I'll make it warm and sunny, your Italian house." She puts on a smile, stroking Ellie's hand.

They split the bill and finish their wine, giddy

about their budding relationship. Ellie feels the
stones that built up in relation to Tatiana chipped
away and crumbled, leaving only the familiar path
of falling in love ahead. She feels indescribable
warmth, imagining everything they get to do
together now, how much simpler their relations
will become.

They begin getting up, picking up their coats
and purses. Ellie confidently takes Tatiana's hand,
and swiftly kisses her lips, beaming with joy.

"Should we go back to my place?" she suggests,
realizing that Tatiana has never actually seen her
house. They slept with each other so many times
in her studio, that she conflated the two in her
mind.

"Sure... it's just that I have my own car." Tatiana
points to it, waiting obediently in the parking lot.
"But I can follow you!" She kisses Ellie's cheek
sweetly.

They get inside the cars, each on her own,
quite entertained by the situation. Ellie drives out
of the parking lot, seeing Tatiana driving in the
rear-view mirror. She's glad to be driving first and
observing, glad to be leading the way, the same
way she often finds herself leading the way within
her relationships. She thinks back to her last rela-

tionship, the way Margaret accused her of wanting to dominate everything in their lives. Those words hurt Ellie deeply at the time, and like a little scar she's been carrying them around ever since, careful to watch herself for any signs that would prove Margaret right. Their relationship died screaming and crying, with many arguments during which both of them said regretful things, but she felt that one sting particularly because she knows a part of it is true. There is a darker side to caring about the other deeply and wanting to arrange everything the best way. She shrugs the unpleasant thoughts away, looking once more to Tatiana, glad to know that she worked on herself and knows better.

11

TATIANA

The sky rolls out its baby blue fabric above, while Tatiana delights in the fresh strawberries she and Ellie brought to the park. Her fingers feel sticky, and she licks them thoroughly before sweetening them once more with the fruits. Children laugh, playing somewhere in the distance, setting up a pleasant, summer-appropriate mood. Tatiana, to celebrate having finished yet another painting in their series, decided to take Ellie out for a picnic in the nearby park, spread widely in the west part of the city.

"As I was saying," Ellie gets back to her point, "nature in this city is miserable."

Tatiana laughs, looking around. Above their

heads trees spread out their rich branches in mazes of leaves, rustling gently with the breeze. The grass spreads out its vibrant green carpet, here and there decorated by blooming bushes. She rolls further away on the soft grass, giving Ellie a long, doubtful look.

"This?" She spreads her arms out, pointing to the abundant nature of the park. "This is miserable to you?"

Ellie shakes her head, apparently unable to convey to Tatiana the richness she experienced growing up close to deep woods. Tatiana looks at her, enchanted by the sensitivity towards her hometown. To a big city person who never really thought of moving away, such a drastic change seemed impressive.

"You'll need to take me sometime, you know," she suggests. "Maybe then I'll understand."

"I should," Ellie nods, in love with the idea of showing Tatiana her home. To roll with her in the untended wild grass, walk along the serpent-like roads slithering ahead in the familiar forests of her youth.

Their afternoon passes slowly, lazily rolling its hours ahead.

"I need to get going soon," Ellie finally announces, getting up from the blanket.

"Alright," Tatiana follows suit, collecting their things. "See you at the studio tomorrow?"

"Sure," Ellie kisses her forehead tenderly.

Tatiana laughs and pulls Ellie closer, laying kisses all over her soft cheeks. Having gathered everything in a particularly disorderly fashion, they head out of the park, holding hands and discussing the differences between the ambience of parks and forests. How something wild becomes tame, a wolf turned into a puppy.

—

Back home, Tatiana's phone rings ceaselessly while she's struggling to unpack her groceries picked up on the way. She bends and twists to reach the phone, dropping a bag of apples on the floor, watching them roll around and clash with each other.

"Yes?" she finally manages to shout.

"Would you like to grab some coffee in about two hours? I have a time slot in the city and nothing to do," Connie says in one breath.

"Pff, sure." Tatiana shrugs, also without any

rigid plans. "Text me the address and I'll be there." She manages to unpack everything and stretch, practicing some of the relaxing techniques Ellie has been telling her about. She doesn't know whether she feels truly relaxed, or simply closer to Ellie, but either way they contribute to her good mood.

—

Once in the I, the two friends plunge right into the details of Tatiana's new collaborative exhibition. She talks excitedly about all the sketches she gave to Ellie to expand upon, and how well she felt painting the ones she got in turn. Then, she mentioned the unfortunate house.

"She did what??" Connie leans over the table in disbelief.

"What? She just asked me to change the colors, that's no big deal," Tatiana explains, surprised by such a harsh reaction.

"No, Tat, she's influencing your style a lot in this exhibition."

Tatiana sits back, perplexed. Ever since beginning the project, she has been more than willing to implement the insignificant changes upon Ellie's requests, but she blamed that exactly on their nature—insignificance. She knew that the project meant more to Ellie than to her, and out of kindness she chose to comply with Ellie's advice. That's what she has been telling herself, each time she would see her art evolve into something new to her. At the end of the day, art is a particularly fluid subject.

"I think maybe we're just inspiring each other," Tatiana says, "that was kind of the point of the project, too."

They both sip on their coffee, watching the sky darken. Tatiana doesn't like the feeling Connie awakened in her, an offense too stinging not to be at least partially true.

"Do you actually think I'm being too soft?" she asks, after a while passes in silence.

"I really do," Connie admits. "I love your bold vision and decisiveness, and also..."

She shifts on the chair, about to say something important.

"What the fuck, tampering with your part of the project? Just leave the house blue," she concludes. Tatiana nods, smiling.

"Just leave the house blue..."

—

On her way to Ellie's studio, Tatiana anxiously grips at the wheel. She knows they're about to have a tense conversation, but she's not shy about her boundaries. After talking to Connie, the house, in particular, began infuriating her. Besides the paintings, why was it always Ellie's studio? She keeps asking herself, rocking to the music coming from the speakers. The summer clouds roll ominously above, dimming the recently strong sun. She takes aggressive turns, disregarding the other cars. She has always been prone to exaggerating her own agitation, quickly spinning into swift conclusions and actions.

She barely manages to stop before a pedestrian crossing, a hair width away from running over an elderly lady. The lady in question shakes her head at Tatiana disapprovingly, then makes her way across the street. A few alleys away from the studio, Tatiana decides to get out of the car and walk the rest of the way.

—

"Hi!" Ellie welcomes her warmly, still tender after their afternoon away at the park.

"Hi." Tatiana enters, upset to be the bringer of a heavy conversation.

"How are you doing?" Ellie closes the door, kissing Tatiana's cheek.

"Yeah... I have something to talk to you about." She sets her things on the table, taking out a colored sketch. It shows a little house somewhere among fields of grape vines, a scene taken out of a dream, a memory, a blend of both, it would seem.

"You see, I think I'll keep the house, the Italian house, remember? I'll keep it in cool tones, because in my opinion it creates an interesting juxtaposition to the surroundings. And we settled on my painting from the sketch that you gave me, and on the sketch there was no indication of color," she states, sure of her words and ready to hear the response.

Ellie nods, upset, apprehensive. She sits down opposite Tatiana, resting her chin on her hands, her eyes set on Tatiana's face.

"Alright, that upsets me, but I feel like you mean to tell me much more than just about the house." She looks at Tatiana, prompting, "You look all on the edge."

This infuriates Tatiana, who already has been feeling talked down to. The apprehensive tone of Ellie's voice doesn't seem to fit the situation, an aggravating attempt at being the bigger person, Tatiana's thoughts sizzle. She feels the burning temptation to make Ellie truly upset. "Well, I think you're influencing me with this project a lot—not your art, which would be fine, but you're giving me a lot of instructions, and it's meant to be a collaboration, not a learning experience for me," she says, ready to elaborate. Ready to throw out all the uncertainty planted by insecurity and watered by Connie's words.

"You also instructed me some, remember?" Ellie asks, innocently, shifting on her chair. "Those were only suggestions! I'd never tell you to recolor a fucking house!" Tatiana shouts.

"Okay, I don't think we have to get so heated about this," Ellie suggests, visibly uncomfortable and unwilling to escalate the situation. She begins playing with her rings, fingering and twisting them one by one, making them sparkle in gold.

Tatiana can see a crossroads ahead, she's driving towards it, full speed. Either to mitigate the situation or to give in to the impulse and pour out all the little ways Ellie has been making her feel

inferior in the recent weeks. The perspective of a
fight tingles her nose, it fills the air between them
with sparks. She doesn't feel as independent
around Ellie as she would like, and she's afraid for
her art. She stands at the crossroads, aggravated,
and takes a step.

"Why are we always painting in your studio,
even?" she fires, spreading out her arms to illus-
trate the point.

"Tatiana, because you do not have a studio," Ellie
responds, rising from her chair. She looks slightly
agitated now, touched either by Tatiana's words or
by Tatiana's intentions, which doesn't matter much
to Tatiana herself. What matters is that she breaks
through this condescending demeanor of Ellie's,
that she gets out her true feelings. She craves
nothing more at the moment but to shatter this
pedestal Ellie is standing on and get her down to the
ground with her, to get her to crawl with anger too.

"I have an apartment," Tatiana accuses.

"And would we just carry the supplies around
from one place to another? Be serious now," Ellie
spreads her arms wide, helpless as to the direction
the conversation is going in.

"Don't tell me to be serious. Don't tell me to be

serious," Tatiana repeats, feeling that the sentence encapsulates her problem exactly. "Who gave you the right to treat me like a child? *Be serious,* for real?" She shakes her head.

Tatiana looks around the studio, feeling her body intensely. Her heart is racing, and her chest is struggling with some tightness she hasn't felt for a long time. Ellie is standing in front of her, and Tatiana has no idea what to feel. She is torn between an impulse to embrace her, and an impulse to run away from the studio and from their relationship.

"I'm sorry." Ellie comes closer.

"Yeah. You're always acting like you know so much better, as if I don't know anything about art or even life, for that matter. Is that what you think? That you need to teach me everything, the way you teach me your little yoga poses?" Tatiana goes on. "It's tiring, Ellie."

She swallows loudly, trying hard not to regret her words, but the feeling leaves a nasty aftertaste in her mouth, sliding down her throat. Regret tastes bitter and stings her tongue.

"Are you tired of me?" Ellie asks, visibly hurt now. She hugs her own shoulders in a nervous gesture, a gesture bringing only more pain to Tatiana.

"Maybe, I don't know. Maybe I am," she utters. "Maybe this project really was a bad idea, and you can't seem to trust me with my own style. Which is just unfair," she concludes.

They stand next to each other for a while, agitated and upset. Tatiana feels a mixture of emotions she cannot untangle from around her throat, tightening her vocal cords and making breathing difficult. She can't be sure whether she meant all the things she said, and her anger seems to be evaporating much quicker than she expected.

"I'm sorry you feel that way," Ellie says, backing further away.

"I think I'll go," Tatiana says under her breath, gathering her things clumsily.

At the door she looks back at Ellie, unsure whether this is the outcome she wanted, but knowing that the little traces of tears around Ellie's eyes would soon burst her heart.

"Bye," she throws into the room, shutting the door behind herself.

On her way home, she begins to feel the avalanche of regret finally overcome her thoughts. As usual, she notices that she started the conversation on the right track, after which she let herself go completely. She rarely takes the right turn on the crossroads, a thing unchanged since childhood.

Her phone rings. She knows it's Ellie so she picks it up.

"Hey, Tatiana." She hears Ellie's voice is slightly raspy, perhaps from crying.

"Hey," Tatiana says carefully, not sure what it is about.

"I thought over some of the things you said, and I think that if you feel this way about me, we shouldn't really be together anymore."

Ellie's voice, hung heavy in the air of Tatiana's small car, rings around her ears ceaselessly. Tatiana focuses her eyes on the road, unsure what she wants to say. Her mind turns into a blank wall, with no wishes and no expectations, only perceiving whatever is about to unravel.

The prolonged silence prompts Ellie to speak again.

"Do you agree? Tatiana?" she asks, her voice shaky and unlike herself.

"I guess so." Tatiana nods to herself. "Yeah, I guess we shouldn't be together then," she adds, unwilling to come off as weak.

"Okay," Ellie says in a quiet voice. "Goodbye, then." She hangs up.

Tatiana's chest tightens, and she stops along the road. The tears come flowing, obscuring her view, blending together colors and lights from the street. She sobs and curses herself for not having tissues, then remembers Ellie always carries tissues around, which prompts her to cry more. She cries half because she's mad at herself for letting the situation be led so far astray, for breaking up in the most ridiculous way she has ever heard, *I guess we shouldn't be together, then,* the word *then* bouncing around her skull like a stubborn balloon. She wipes her eyes with her sleeves, determined to get home. On her way, she calls Connie—the two have rekindled their frequent conversations—and Tatiana turns into an incorrigible talker when unhappy with herself.

"Yes darling?" Connie responds, infallible, "Are you driving?"

"I am," Tatiana says in the same shrill voice she heard Ellie use only a minute ago. "I just broke my own heart," she cries.

"What do you mean, what happened? Did you break up?"

Tatiana bites her lip, unhappy with how harsh the word sounds.

"I think we just did," she confesses.

—

Back home, she realizes how unfortunately timed her breakup with Ellie is. Their project is still ongoing, with the vernissage of the exhibition set for a date three weeks ahead. She realizes, also, that one of her canvases was left at Ellie's studio. She collapses onto a chair, exhausted and dreading the organizational difficulties. Maybe love is just finely clothed desire, she reflects back on Connie's words, unsure how to even begin processing the situation. She gets her laptop out, thinking that maybe she should disclose her ideas as to organizing the last bits of preparation before the exhibition to Ellie by email, retaining a formal tone and keeping it brief. She figures Ellie is probably not in the mood to hear from her, so she decides to write it and schedule it to be sent one day from now. *Ridiculous,* she keeps repeating in her thoughts, cursing herself for not thinking things through.

In the middle of writing the email, she realizes

these details keep her from fully feeling the weight of the breakup on her shoulders. There is no *I miss how soft her lips felt against mine,* nothing of the *when she kissed my forehead that one time I thought I would never know more tenderness* sort. There's only:

Hi Ellie, related to our upcoming exhibition;

Things I would like to get back from the studio:

- *My canvas (unfinished painting)*
- *My set of brushes*
- *My paint*

Keep me updated about your progress by mail.

Kind regards,

Tatiana

And the message is safely deposited in the mysterious category of "to be delivered," out of sight, out of mind. Tatiana shuts her laptop close, but soon opens it once more, deciding to go on a spending spree. Rather, she doesn't *decide* to go on a spending spree, she submits to the river current of her usual response towards heartbreak; she doesn't resist the appeal of the rush of happiness. She decides she's in need of jewelry, in need of antique decor, and in desperate, pulsing need of summer dresses. Now that she's single, she needs to look her best—that was the common wisdom shared in her college dorm, wisdom she carried well into her adult years.

Looking through vintage silhouettes and pre-loved shining bracelets, she suddenly gets very tired. Sighing, she postpones the purchases, deciding to go to bed early. Her mother used to say that most of people's troubles are connected solely to their minds. *Just go to sleep, dear,* she would say. *The morning thoughts flow clearer.*

With this advice in mind, Tatiana takes a long, excruciatingly hot shower. She lets the weight of the day go from her shoulders, massaged by the water. She tries letting her thoughts flow freely, though quietly and gently. The dim bathroom light envelopes her figure, and for a moment, she feels comforted to be alone.

Laying down to sleep, her eyes water. To the beat of memories of Ellie's laughter, she weeps herself to sleep.

12

ELLIE

Ellie packs for the trip lightly. She double-checks the train's details, knowing how chaotic her friends are capable of getting. She has always been described as the "mother friend," and whenever she isn't the one to plan everything out, she's certain it will go disastrously. She's been recently trying to work on this impulse, though, which is partially why she agreed to go on the mountain trip. Besides, it offers a short escape from the city, a chance to reconnect with nature, and a chance to clear her thoughts. She nods, proud of herself for finally getting away from the recently suffocating city.

A few days ago, she got Tatiana's email, which more than anything made her laugh. Then it made her cry, then it made her respond in that same, ridiculously casual, formal tone. The email exchange, really, was the deciding factor in her agreeing to the trip, she finally admits.

Fred and his fiancé, Thomas, opted out of it at the last moment, much to Ellie's relief.

She rolls the last pair of socks and places them firmly in her backpack. There's a certain levity included in not having to overthink her clothes, the unending choices made to contribute to a coherent image. In the mountains, everyone looks the same. Sweaty, muddy, wearing unflattering sportswear.

–

On her way to the station, Ellie soaks in the realization that she hasn't seen most of these people for over a year. She fell out of touch with most due to work, their marriages and children, their routines that no longer fit Ellie in. The lack of anyone truly close to her makes the perspective both exciting and frightening, mostly because the group will have no context for her recent emotional state. The state in question has been fluctuating, mainly between Ellie feeling powerful and proud of her communication skills, heart-broken over losing Tatiana, and a strange mixture of both. A strange sense of preventability and futility of their argument, as if the issue could've been resolved. She hates feeling this way, usually the person who avoids arguments until they're unavoidable and necessary. Was it the case?

Before the departure of her train, she decides to quickly call home and check up on her mother. Busy preparing the exhibition, she missed some of their weekly calls. Looking for a free parking spot, she waits on the line.

"Hey Mom," she says, getting out of the car. "How have you been?"

"Oh hi, darling!" Her mother's voice seems to betray a slight surprise, but she beams with happiness regardless. "You know, better and worse. The wonderful Mr. Keith is taking care of me, together with Dad, of course," her mother's tone sounds weak, but Ellie can swear that it's stronger than the last time.

"That's good to hear, Mom," Ellie says, thinking that later she'll email Keith to send over any relevant details. "How's Dad doing?"

"Oh, he's just outside, gardening. You know how focused he gets, cutting his flowers and what-not," her mother brightens up, "And how are you, is everything alright?"

Ellie looks at the departures board, having her mother's voice in her earphones and texting the trip group chat simultaneously, nervous whether they'll make it to the train.

"Ah, you know," she sighs, "ups and downs. I need a break from the city; I'm going to the mountains for a few days with friends."

"Have fun," her mother responds, with a tinge of knowing in her voice.

"Listen, I called just to check up on you, but I need to run now, so bye and talk soon!"

"Bye bye, Sweetie." Ellie hangs up.

Her friends are waiting on the platform. She turns her phone over and over in her hand, disappointed by the conversation with her mother. She knows that sometimes she calls to hear some soothing semblance of comfort in her mom's voice, but she's not a child anymore, for a long time she hasn't been, and her mother more often than not cannot provide her with what she needs. Perhaps mountains will, she shrugs, making her way to the platform.

She soon finds that her friends' jolly moods are not as infectious as she had wished. She begins sulking in her seat, unable to relate to their little stories and jokes. Understanding that something is clearly troubling her, her friends decide to give her space, which only ends up being alienating. Ellie feels stuck, listening to the train's steady rhythm.

Once arrived, the group takes to hiking with no time to lose. Their hut is almost at the top of the mountain, and no one feels in the mood to hike in the dark. Giving herself over to her own body's rhythm, Ellie finds solace for a while. She pays attention to her heart's steady beating, her breathing strained—a witness to her efforts. The quiet crunch of leaves below her shoes reminds her of running laps around the forest as a teenager, her favorite way to deal with difficult feelings back then. First loves, first losses of friendships, first disappointments—she flows from memory to memory, face to face. Some are more faded than others, some left a significant mark, while others she thought would leave one didn't. She laughs at herself a bit, how she thought then that relationships would get easier, when they really never did.

"Ellie, are you fine?" Anabelle calls to her, and she notices she's been dragging behind the group.

She quickens her step, determined to get to the hut soon.

Upon arriving at the beautifully hidden away hut, surrounded by trees, its foreground peppered with wide benches, Ellie feels relieved. She deposits her bag in the room, then gets out to get some fresh air and admire the dusk coming over the rich forest. Her friends stayed inside, chatting over pints of beer, tired and united in their hike.

Ellie looks at the burgeoning night sky, the hint of silver beginning by a multitude of stars. Stars she's been missing ever since moving to the city. Their ancient glimmer has a soothing quality, but she doesn't feel soothed. She realizes she feels full of sorrow.

This sorrow does not feel finite. It is not grief, she suspects; it is something still warm and buzzing. Tatiana's words, on repeat in Ellie's head throughout the day, felt insincere and wavering. They felt unfinished, tangled. Out of the sorrow emerges a faint thread of hope, hope perhaps best reinforced by a beer. She gets up from the bench and directs her steps inside, craving a drink. Her friends seem occupied with themselves, laughing at some joke told before she entered. She smiles at them and grabs a drink, leaves once more to sit enveloped by the grandeur of the landscape and the current of hope carrying her thoughts towards hurried solutions.

Before she realizes, she's holding her phone, looking for Tatiana's number. Before she has time to think, she's calling.

And waiting.

Receiving no response. Only the cold, steady sound of a rejected connection.

Disheartened, she runs her thoughts back to the argument, rolling Tatiana's words around her mind. Ellie knows her tendency to come off as slightly controlling. Or, whatever, arrogant. These accusations always stun her, not as something untrue, but absurd. She loves to take great care of those dear to her, lovers, friends, or family. The idea that she will actually have to put work into this side of her, if she wants to be with someone like Tatiana, forms slowly but sturdily.

She picks up the phone again, not ready to apologize but warming up to the idea at the back of her mind.

Rejected.

She finishes her beer and realizes she's beginning to get cold, beginning to feel desolate. Two unanswered calls are enough to make her look desperate, and she holds that knowledge painfully. Despite feeling degraded, she tries again.

Fails.

She decides to go to sleep. Walking back to the hut, she decides to put the thoughts about Tatiana to stop for the duration of the trip. Then, reaching the doorknob she changes her mind. She's going to think thoroughly about herself in relation to Tatiana. When they get the chance to talk again, she will be ready to face the situation. She will be ready to rekindle their connection and start anew, with a better foundation.

She passes the laughing crowd of friends and heads downstairs to try to sleep. The little dark room seems to her more of a wooden cave, but she doesn't mind. Its cool temperature seems perfect to simply slip into the sheets and drift away to sleep. She's craving the deep, dreamless sleep of a child, the black abyss able to comfort a mind, instead of the shallow, feverish sleep full of haunting dreams. She brushes her teeth, feeling the wave of tiredness rise up her legs. Lying down to sleep, enveloped by the sheets, her mind is only able to focus on Tatiana's face, her laughter, her soft fingertips that used to trace Ellie's face. Then she remembers the burning words thrown at her by

Tatiana, the undeserved anger filling the space of her studio, a space previously filled by countless confessions and laughter. She lies quietly, unable to comprehend the reason for such an outburst and suddenly glad that Tatiana didn't pick up. The situation was not only Ellie's fault, and she knows that she would have burst out in apologies instead of acting more reasonably. Plagued by thoughts of this nature, she slowly drifts away into a restless sleep.

13

TATIANA

The hairbrush keeps fishing out small tangles in Tatiana's long unruly red hair. She pushes it down with more strength, ripping out a few strands. Today is her grand vernissage—she only learned *how* grand the vernissage is going to be very recently—and it is marked by her hair being in horrible condition. Otherwise, she feels at peace. When she forces every thought of Ellie far away from the track of her thoughts, she feels at peace.

The last few days, Tatiana has been contemplating the collection deeply. She looked through all the artwork combined, Ellie's and her own, and thought it to be a truly perfect blend. Feeling confident about the art allows her to be in her element during the opening.

While getting dressed, she finally has to admit, as well; the unanswered calls, still somewhere at the back of her mind, give her some additional confidence. A little ego-boost, a taste in her mouth so sweet she can almost ignore its sickly aftertaste. At the time, she regretted profusely leaving them abandoned, she craved hearing Ellie again, maybe even apologizing, which does not come to her easily. But now, she feels over the affair—this she repeats like a mantra. She feels excited to open her exhibition and lets herself be proud of the work that went into it.

—

Uncharacteristically exactly on time, Tatiana finds the perfect parking spot, almost by the entrance. Gathering herself, she sits for a while behind the wheel, watching the early guests enter. Some friends, some journalists. When she catches a glimpse of Ellie's figure by the entrance, she freezes. Tatiana realizes that she hasn't seen Ellie in person since the argument. Her things from the studio were brought to her by Fred, all the details settled by email. The feelings she thought were dealt with suddenly resurface, flooding her calm demeanor with a storm. The winds of memories tug at her confidence, waves of longing storm the shores of her stoic approach to the situation. The same figure that used to embrace Tatiana warmly, kiss her lips tenderly, laugh with her for hours— that same figure is standing right there, talking to someone, smiling invitingly. Tatiana makes an effort to push these unruly feelings back down, deciding this is not the time nor space for a dissection of her romantic situation. She is going there as a professional artist, looking to present her work and forge new connections, she tells herself, feigning confidence. She is going there as a professional artist, who would never hook up in a gallery's bathroom, she smirks to herself going up the stairs.

She can see Ellie handling some introductions and tries not to think too hard about it. She will only try to keep her distance, as naturally as possible. The assistants walk around with trays full of glasses, swift and graceful. Tatiana turns around, looking at the works of art hanging, gloriously, on the walls. She feels proud, truly proud of herself and of Ellie, whatever relationship they may have now, for completing such a big project together. In a moment, the time to make the opening speech together will come, and in preparation Tatiana decides to drink up one glass. There aren't many guests yet, everything stands half-full. It's difficult to perform this dance of avoiding Ellie at all costs, a dance that she's been dancing for a while, with only half of the room full. She didn't make a conscious decision to avoid Ellie; in truth, she thought herself over the situation, capable of having a casual chat with her. That turned out not to be the case at all, as if around Ellie grew an electric field, able to shock her and tangle all the particles inside of Tatiana. Once they get on stage, her proximity will be unavoidable, she realizes. Her citrus scent and the quiet dangling of her earrings will be just a few steps away, certain to tease her memory and stir some deeply hidden sense of regret. A group approaches her, and she is infinitely grateful for the offered distraction. They ask about the process, the art of collaboration, the purpose. It's a group of students writing an article on the importance of artistic collaboration, and they are desperate to get a quick interview. Tatiana agrees and tells them her perspective.

"Art forms like painting can be very individualistic, which has a good and a bad side. I think it's wonderful to see a singular person's vision, just laid out on the canvas, but of course, there are downsides of always creating alone."

"What did you find the most rewarding, painting the project with someone else?"

Tatiana looks around, subconsciously looking for Ellie.

"Oh, well... One can definitely learn much from the experience. Possibly gain a new perspective to view one's own art, one's own approach." She nods. "It all depends on the pair, to be honest. I think collaborations are something we should practice from time to time, to diversify our artistic experience."

She excuses herself after this conclusion, feeling a slight distaste towards her words. She doesn't believe that an artist necessarily *should* be doing anything. The only responsibility of the artist, in her mind, is to do their art justice.

She half-heartedly engages in conversation here and there, checking her watch frequently to see how much time she has left until the dreaded speech. The hall is slowly filling up, relaxing her nerves a little. The sea of people dressed fashionably flows beneath her paintings, and the scene looks quite glamorous, making her smile.

At last, the time comes.

Ellie and Tatiana make their way to the slightly elevated part of the room, and the light focuses on them sharply. For a moment, it seems as if the world is beyond the two, in the halo of light, Tatiana stands singled out with Ellie against the mass of shadow-covered figures, and time seems to slow down for a moment. She feels a spark of desire to take Ellie's hand for encouragement, followed by the sobering realization of their current estrangement. Both of them seem to have been dancing the same dance, both avoiding each other's gaze, passing around only a quiet hello. The entire affair seems hopeless to Tatiana, something gooey and unpleasant.

Ellie begins the speech, something they outlined together to be concise and to the point.

"We want to thank everyone who made this exhibition possible, especially George Kirsch," here she points to George, and a round of applause fills the space for a moment, "and the wonderful staff of the gallery."

Here Tatiana takes over. She clears her throat before elaborating upon their project's vision.

"We had the honor of being approached by Mister Kirsch, due to the rising interest in our work—something we're infinitely grateful for. The idea is simple: to expand our artistic horizons, we completed each other's old, unrealized sketches. The process proved *strenuous*," she couldn't help but give Ellie a glance, "but after all, we're both proud of our work and excited to let you explore it for yourselves. Enjoy your evening!" she finishes the brief speech, showered by a thunder of applause. Ellie and Tatiana nod their heads courteously, then disperse once more into the crowd, floating away from each other with a subtle urgency in their steps.

Walking around, Tatiana notices a group of young artists gathered around one of the paintings. She approaches, curious to hear their opinions. The painting is one of Ellie's, depicting one of the swimming pool scenes. It's a pastel-colored affair, large swaths of delicate blue enveloping a little girl. Her swimming cap is dreamy pink, matching the pinkish skin tone. She stands at the edge of the pool, looking down at the glistening water, pondering whether to jump in. The painting grips Tatiana's heart a little, seeing the characteristic brush strokes around the pool's edges, softening their harsh corners. Ellie painted this work while they were still together, and Tatiana remembers distinctly painting something right next to it. Ellie joked about the little girl looking a bit like a shrimp with all the pink tones, and they both laughed for ages about it.

To get her thoughts away from Ellie, she finally gets closer to the group to listen into their conversation.

"I like the juxtaposition of the pink with blue," says some girl, not older than twenty. "I think the girl looks like she's about to move, which adds a certain dynamism to the piece."

Overall, Tatiana gathers positive feedback, and leaves the gathering to their own devices. She realizes that she's cruising and decides that the only way to stop the useless floating around is to finally have a conversation with Ellie. Otherwise, she will spend the whole evening dabbling in the weird mixture of craving to see her and avoiding it at all cost; a pathetic state she wants a way out of. She takes a deep breath, and bravely seeks Ellie out in the crowd.

In her way suddenly stands Fred.

"Tatiana! I haven't seen you in so long," he says as they embrace warmly. "I simply adore the paintings. Will elaborate soon, for now—how have you been, for Christ's sake?"

"Oh, you know," Tatiana sighs, a bit ashamed of getting out of touch with him. He is the person she associates the strongest with Ellie, so talking has been difficult.

"Anyway," Fred says, perhaps intuiting it to not be the best moment for conversation, "I'm looking for Thomas, I lost him somewhere. If you want to know, Ellie is in the corner over there." He points to the other end of the room and winks. It's clear that he wants to see the two back together.

Of course she's at the other end of the room, Tatiana thinks to herself, shaking her head. Ellie can be unreasonable and infuriating, but her ever-flowing sensitivity would always bring out something soft in Tatiana. Something tender, like the kisses they shared in her brightly lit studio. She walks along the walls exhibiting the fruits of their artistic union; her ideas painted by Ellie's hand seem so intimate and embraced, they seem complete. Even though their idea was simple, it birthed something truly beautiful, both conceptually and visually. Her eyes feast on the sight for a moment, letting the crowd roll around in the foreground.

She spots Ellie's head from afar. Making her way towards the spectacularly dressed figure, she can feel her heart sink a bit deeper with anxiety, but she keeps on walking regardless. She's determined to focus on her feelings and let them speak, instead of eluding them like usual. The two exchange glances, and she nods for Ellie to come over. They haven't truly spoken to each other in three weeks, and standing face to face, the atmosphere feels tense. Tatiana clears her throat, trying not to let Ellie's eyes distract her.

"Hey, Ellie," she begins, "Congratulations on the exhibition."

Ellie looks at her a little suspiciously but responds in a kind tone.

"Congratulations to you too," she says.

They begin smirking, the corners of their mouths dancing. Tatiana can feel the warmth they recently shared rekindle almost instantly, diminishing the built-up distance between them. So strange, she thinks, the way she simply feels at home when hearing Ellie's voice so close, no matter the circumstances. They look around the crowd, as if to find a neutral anchor to tie their conversation around.

"Lots of people here," Tatiana adds in a casual,

inviting tone. Her muscles relax, and she feels like she's floating atop the current of their conversation, not trying to control anything, and not trying to seem artificially indifferent. She is not indifferent. She feels each word deeply.

"True. We must be pretty good painters," Ellie says, and they giggle at the miserably bad joke. That's the beauty, though, the way they don't require much to make each other smile, throwing around bad jokes just to make the other laugh.

"I think you're a pretty good painter, Ellie," Tatiana shifts her tone towards something a little more sincere. A little more open, hinting at a willingness to actually talk. She feels relieved that their current conversation doesn't revolve around the breakup, as if being suspended above their recent falling out.

"I..." Ellie seems to notice the shift. "Thank you, that means a lot. I mean it."

She looks to the painting closest to them, one of Tatiana's.

"You know... I never, ever, wanted to make you feel like a lesser artist, or a lesser person—" she smirks, remembering, "Alright, maybe the first time we met, perhaps a little bit then."

They both share a quiet laugh, reminiscing

about the dinner that set everything in motion. The way their argument sparked something between the two, perhaps being the exact reason why they feel so drawn to each other. One form of heat can birth another, it seems.

"Mhm." Tatiana nods, eager to see where the chat takes them. She feels reassured, less by the words and more so by Ellie's intentions. It seems she actually put effort into thinking how her actions affected Tatiana. At least that's what Tatiana hopes to learn.

"I want you to know, that whatever happens, we might go our separate ways, or stay friends—" Ellie's voice breaks a little, she glances at Tatiana to see whether the break was noticeable. Tatiana doesn't betray that it was.

She feels something gluey and heavy in her chest, thinking about being friends with Ellie. Imagining that she would have to see her around and not be able to give her a quick kiss, invite her over and fall asleep entangled together in a loving mess, or take her out on dates that would turn into hours upon hours of conversations. This mud in her chest weighs her down, drowning out any words she might've wanted to say as a response.

"Either way," Ellie continues, "I want you to

know that I cherish you very, very deeply as a person, and I will work on myself for you no matter in what way you'll remain in my life," she stops before saying the unimaginable, "if you decide to remain in it at all."

Tatiana turns her head away, afraid of crying in the middle of her exhibition, afraid that if she keeps looking at Ellie she actually might. The words touched her to the core, and now, hugging her own shoulders, she has no idea what to do with herself.

"Can you hug me?" she asks before she has the chance to think it through.

Ellie's green eyes soften, and she takes a step towards Tatiana. Her perfume overwhelms Tatiana's senses, reminding her of the many nights they shared, welcoming sleep in a mutual embrace. She extends her face a little and touches Ellie's lips, only slightly, only a gentle brush.

"What are you doing, dear?" Ellie asks, looking around, nervous.

The guests assumed it only natural for the pair of artists to be emotional at the culmination point of their collaboration, and a faint drizzle of applause greets them. Ellie and Tatiana began nodding with appreciation, silently laughing to themselves about the context of the situation. They disentangle themselves from each other, exchanging looks with various friends watching, bowing a little to the journalists and art collectors.

"We just can't stay away from each other at exhibitions, huh?" Tatiana says.

"So it seems." Ellie shakes her head.

They spend the rest of the night conversing with the guests, telling little anecdotes about their work, and making new connections in the world of art. The lightness they both got from their conversation proved very useful during the exhibition. For both, the event will necessarily bring much publicity in the upcoming weeks, further accelerating their careers, offering a string of exciting opportunities. Tatiana feels on top of the world, from time to time turning her head to discreetly watch Ellie. She feels every handshake of Ellie's, and every smile, with a deep sense of untamed affection. A sea of longing to reunite waves about her head, a thing she has no idea how to deal with later, once they part, once they go back to their single lives. She simply allows herself to feel everything tonight, to get carried by her feelings and see where they take her. Taming them, she realizes, will only make her bitter and unpleasant to be around. Taming them will only prove full of strain.

The gallery slowly empties, and their acquaintances group around them, asking impatiently about an afterparty. Ellie and Tatiana made sure to think it through before and reserved a table at a nearby club. Both, however, could read in each other's eyes a growing hesitation. They let everyone know the address and said that they need to finish gathering their things at the gallery.

"We'll join soon," Ellie reassures everyone.

Once the group is out the door, Tatiana is all over Ellie's lips. They drink away from each other all the uncertainty and miscommunication, they feed each other with thirst for something sincere and uncomplicated. Their bodies have been craving each other for a long time.

"We should get the hell away from here," Tatiana whispers to Ellie's ear.

"True," Ellie agrees, and they leave the gallery.

The air outside is crisp and fragrant, the park nearby spreads the various scents of summer around. The street is entirely empty.

"Let's walk for a minute," Ellie suggests.

"Sure."

They walk, holding hands. Their pace is slow

and appreciative of the evening, but something clearly hangs between the two women. Tatiana understands that to simply go back to their old ambiguous relationship is not something either one would want.

"Let me say something," Tatiana begins. "I came to you that afternoon in a rush, right after a conversation with my friend. She really hyped me up to confront you about that silly house painting. I'm not saying she was wrong. I think what you did really upset me," she stops for a moment to think the following words through. "But I was never even imagining breaking up," she confesses. "I didn't want to look like a fool later when you suggested it, so I simply agreed. That was dumb."

She stops and takes up Ellie's hands. Their warmth only encourages her to continue, the pulsing skin of her beloved.

"I truly care about you. Tonight, I felt so silly. I was just walking around half-scared, half-craving to see you."

Ellie laughs gently.

"I was doing the same thing," she admits, kissing Tatiana lightly on the lips.

"I think," Tatiana gets to the less pleasant part, "I think that if we commit to changing certain things... I definitely need to work on my anger, for example," she breathes in, shakily, "but I think that if we work hard, we will do well as a couple. I would like us to do well as a couple."

Ellie nods, visibly relieved.

"I would like that very much."

They embrace tightly, not letting each other go. Tatiana begins rocking them side to side, in a calming motion. She gets closer to Ellie's ear.

"Do you want to go back to my place?" she asks.

"I do," Ellie answers, grinning into Tatiana's hair.

They get into Tatiana's car, and drive through the emptying streets.

"Oh my god," Ellie sighs, "We forgot about the afterparty."

"I didn't forget about anything," Tatiana answers casually, "I wasn't going there."

They laugh and let the simple joy of sitting next to each other fill them up entirely.

—

Once home, they begin kissing before either has even the chance to take off her shoes. The emotional turbulence they have endured throughout the day melts softly into a rain of sizzling desire, plump with tenderness and longing. Ellie begins taking off Tatiana's coat, lips still locked together. Tatiana chuckles.

"Let me take off my shoes, darling," she whispers, for a moment letting herself out of their tight embrace.

They take off their coats, their shoes, lay down their purses. Each motion carries with it the delicate scent of the night's gentle seductions. They're careful not to cause abrupt noise, two performers in the house of desire.

Tatiana takes Ellie by her hand and leads her to the bedroom. The window, left slightly ajar, lets gentle breeze into the room. Ellie brushes hair from Tatiana's face, laying kisses on her forehead, cheeks, finally getting to her lips and playfully teasing with her tongue.

The women lock once more in a kiss, this time less gentle and more fiery, they're almost feasting on each other's lips, taking off their dresses, and hungrily falling towards the bed.

Tatiana can feel her legs getting impatient, the blissful tingling around her thighs makes her cling to Ellie tighter, feeling her skin against her own in an act of confirmation—she will get what she wants, sooner or later. They delight in their bodies fitting into one another, their ancient dance feels fated, embraced by the moony glimpses of night.

Ellie is on top, sliding down Tatiana's body to lick her nipples with a teasing lightness. Tatiana's hips grind, unashamed to show how badly she wants to be touched, to be possessed by Ellie's hands, tongue, mouth, only to be had by Ellie. She begins to tremble lightly with anticipation, at first determined to tame it, but after a while giving in entirely.

"Oh, I see what your legs are doing," Ellie whispers, laying her hand in between Tatiana's thighs, still in her underwear. She keeps on licking her nipples, while her hand holds Tatiana's pussy steadily and in no rush to take off the underwear, feeling the material get more and more wet. Tatiana's hips force themselves stronger against Ellie's touch, pleading.

"Please," she whispers.

"Of course, darling," Ellie responds, laying her lips once more against Tatiana's, and sliding her underwear down. She moans with pleasure a little, feeling how deliciously wet and ready Tatiana's pussy is. She feels every part of her vulva, then begins circling around her opening. Her fingers are still a bit cold, making Tatiana shiver a little.

"Do you want me inside?" Ellie asks, teasing.

Her fingers begin sliding in, only an inch, only half a fingertip in, then they slide out immediately. This sets Tatiana's body aflame, desperate to finally get fucked.

"I do, I do," she nods, her eyebrows tightly knit and mouth open. "Please fuck me," she begs.

"Alright." Ellie slides in three fingers, feeling Tatiana's pussy stretch to accommodate her. Tatiana gasps in her delightful moaning voice, glazed by bliss.

"Oh yes, please," she moans, setting her legs wider apart.

"Good, good girl," Ellie whispers into Tatiana's ear.

She keeps the steady rhythm that always brings Tatiana to the shivering, head twisting moment. Then once she is there, she pushes the rest of her hand inside Tatiana just like she did that first time. She grabs Tatiana's wrists and puts them above her head, which lets little whimpers out of Tatiana's mouth, nicely open and soft.

"Keep your hands there," Ellie commands.

Tatiana begins moaning louder, putting her thighs together, twisting away.

"Tatiana look at me," Ellie says, a little out of breath. "Open your legs," she commands.

Tatiana does what she's told, feeling on the edge. Ellie's hand knows the rhythm and is restlessly working, bringing Tatiana to tears.

Tatiana knows she is close, very close. She feels a finger from Ellie's other hand teasing her anus and she feels overwhelmed with her own excitement.

Ellie owning her body and fucking her every which way excites her like nothing else.

"Please..uh.." she moans as Ellie's finger pushes deep inside her ass and it feels like the most incredible thing she can imagine.

"Come on, come for me," Ellie says gently.

"Can I?"

"Yes you can." Ellie fucks her a bit more strongly, making Tatiana cry out, tensing up her thighs and face.

Tatiana feels all her nerves tied up and twisted around Ellie's hand and finger stretching her pussy and her ass. Then, she feels her orgasm building and building unit it tips over the edge and crashes around her; she relaxes her legs, looking sheepishly at Ellie. For a moment, they don't say anything, only curl up together under the sheets, breathing heavily and holding each other's sweaty bodies.

Tatiana gets very sleepy, a habit they both used to laugh about as something likening her to a man after her orgasm,

"I'm so sleepy," she yawns. "That felt good."

"That felt very good," Ellie kisses her forehead, feeling slightly tired as well.

"I love you," Tatiana murmurs, hopefully.

"I love you, too." Ellie smiles and her smile is like the sunshine.

"I think I need to shower, though."

"Yes, let's shower," Tatiana decides, shaking her head to wake up and starting to get up from the bed. They enter the bathroom, laying gentle kisses on each other's lips. Ellie takes Tatiana in her arms in the hot stream of water, and they stay that way for a while, simply feeling each other breathe, feeling the subtle movement of each other's chests. They share a very wet kiss, bathed by the abundance of water and comfort, leaning on the shower's wall. They can read from each other's eyes the feeling of being home.

EPILOGUE

4 YEARS LATER

Ellie keeps looking for the little wooden horse, digging through the backpack's pockets with a diligence previously unknown to her. She slides her fingers attentively into every crevice in the fabric, to no avail.

"I really can't find it, Tatiana!" she shouts, hoping that her voice will find its way upstairs.

Shaking her head, she lays the little bag aside. Parenthood has taught her the strangest of lessons, making her see how subjective significance can be. They have been looking for the horse for an hour now, digging through every possible place, every bag, every room, unable to console the cries of their treasured boy. She can hear Elijah cry again, and the shrill sound makes her heart twist. There might be no remedy but to buy a new horse, but neither she nor Tatiana remembered where the thing was from.

She makes her way upstairs, kicking aside some leftover boxes. Even though they moved in over a month ago, unpacking has been dragging on endlessly, overshadowed by the day-to-day affairs of the three. Ever since having Elijah, their already hectic lives went spinning at a speed neither one could have predicted but that both appreciate.

Ellie leans on the doorframe of Elijah's room, looking at Tatiana gently rocking him in her arms, calming down his nerves. Seeing this view never fails to make Ellie feel swelled with love. The little boy's soft head rests against Tatiana's chest, he yawns, tired of crying.

"I think he's more nervous than usual because of the trip," Ellie says, quietly. "He can sense that we're stressed."

She comes closer to where Tatiana is sitting, and carefully begins to stroke Elijah's hair. His little curls feel like a tangle of clouds to her, and as she slowly spreads her fingers into them, the boy smiles sleepily. Tatiana and Ellie look at each other, dark circles surround their love-ridden eyes. They rock on the floor together for a little while, enjoying a moment of quiet on the thick children's carpet.

"I think I know where the horse is," Tatiana says in a whisper, afraid to wake Elijah up.

"Where?"

"Remember when I took him swimming?" She sighs. "I think we must've lost it there."

Ellie nods, content at least to be able to stop searching. They fall back into the bliss of silence, forehead against forehead in a constellation of love. Their boy stirs around some, with the clumsy movements little children make, as if unadjusted yet to the hands they'd been given. Tatiana lays him in his bed, and they tiptoe out of the room, leaving the door slightly ajar.

"You know," Ellie begins, "we should finally unpack all these boxes in the corridor."

They descend the stairs, tired, but still tingling with happiness.

"After Rome," says Tatiana. "We'll take care of it when we're back."

They go to the kitchen and, through the big window in the middle, they can see heavy clouds birth strings of summer rain. The hot ground in touch with the freezing water breathes some steam, causing the scene to look almost apocalyptic. Ellie and Tatiana both tense up, looking at each other, waiting for Elijah to wake up due to the noise. Not hearing anything, they slowly come to relax again. Enveloped in the warmth of their home, they observe the falling rain. Ellie feels ensconced, as if hidden away in a different universe than the cruel, cold outside world. She hopes Tatiana shares the feeling, and as if seeking confirmation, she takes up her hand. Holding her, Ellie knows.

They boil water for some tea, wishing to relax before packing for the long journey that awaits them. Soft silence welcomes them, the steady noise of boiling water rocks their senses gently. Ellie brings Tatiana closer into her arms, feeling the copper hair against her face. They rest in each other's arms, taking in the calm atmosphere the evening unexpectedly graced them with.

Suddenly, the pillow-like silence is cut through by the phone's ringing. They reluctantly pull away from each other, and Tatiana reaches to pick up the call.

"It's Mister Bianchi," she says to Ellie before picking up. "Hi, Mister Bianchi. It's Tatiana Khan speaking, yes."

Ellie listens in to the steady flow of words,

words with a distinct Italian rhythm, rustling in between the speaker and Tatiana's ear. She cannot hear what is being said, and is quite content Tatiana chose to speak, for she can feel her own head grow leaden with exhaustion.

"Oh." Tatiana makes circles around the kitchen, the way she always does when talking on the phone. Her legs pick up the pace of the conversation. "Well, that would be very generous of you, of course, of course..."

Ellie sits down, waiting patiently to hear the details. She places her weary head in her hands, free to observe Tatiana's body language, her beloved hands and the little frowning of her face from focus. Since moving in, they have had little time to spend entirely alone, and moments like these allow Ellie to truly let the love for Tatiana spill onto her every thought. The trip to Rome is a tremendous professional opportunity, but she admits to herself that she mainly wants to spend time with Tatiana and their son, for a moment away from the bustling life they lead here, a life for which she nonetheless is grateful every day. Rome awaits them, in all its glorious beauty, and even more so, it awaits to welcome their art to one of its galleries. And once they get to know life in the

Italian city, they will move on to savor the land's countryside. They will have all the time in the world, learning to live slowly and in bliss, until finally getting to miss their home, and full of memories, they will make their way back.

Tatiana hangs up, beaming with happiness. Ellie cannot help smiling, seeing her like that.

"Guess what!" she exclaims, then remembering Elijah is sleeping quiets down. "Guess what."

"I won't guess." Ellie shakes her head, knowing she truly would not. "Tell me everything."

"Bianchi is offering to cover all transportation-related costs," she spits out in one breath. "This literally takes away like half of the expenses we were accounting for."

Ellie nods, letting the sentences sink in. The evening seems so dreamy to her that any concrete piece of information takes a long time to appear in her mind as real and tangible.

"That's wonderful," she says, looking at Tatiana.

"Why are you looking at me like this?" Tatiana chuckles, very visibly relieved by the offer.

"I love you," Ellie confesses, simply.

That's all that is left on her mind, in the warm lights of their kitchen, shielded from the storm outside, whispering not to wake their little son up. The unadorned confession is the only thing reverberating around her thoughts, bumping around like a ball being kicked into infinity. Looking into Tatiana's bright eyes, still glimmering even despite the exhaustion, looking at her lips forming a gentle smile, and thinking that this is the person she gets to build a family with—the only thing on her mind is love.

"Oh, you!" Tatiana pulls Ellie up, into her arms. "I love you too, darling."

They share a long and tender kiss, before a clap of thunder erupts and wakes Elijah up.

"I'll get him downstairs to sit with us, what do you think?" Ellie asks.

She climbs the stairs to remedy the sleepy boy's troubles, finding him sitting on the bed and weeping.

"Mommy I'm scared, scared," he keeps mumbling, clutching his blanket in tight fists.

"Oh darling, come here," Ellie takes him up in her arms, feeling the warm forehead rest against her skin. He reaches for the back of her neck, allowing himself to sink into the comfort of his mother's tender arms.

She carries him downstairs, gently stroking his

small head, whispering sweet things to make him forget the sudden noise of thunder. Tatiana puts on a calm jazz piece, and the music, akin to a tender lover's lullaby, fills their living room. She comes up to them, and embracing Ellie with Elijah in between, she initiates a slow, loving dance. Moving step by step, rocking a little to the soothing saxophone, they circle the room. They dance his tearfulness away, lulling him to sleep, the music drowns out the simmering sounds of falling rain, and they might keep on dancing so through the entire night.

FREE BOOK

I really hope you enjoyed this story. I loved writing it.

I'd love for you to get my FREE book- Her Boss- by joining my mailing list. On my mailing list you can be the first to find out about free or discounted books or new releases and get short sexy stories for free! Just click on the following link or type into your web browser: https://BookHip. com/MNVVPBP

Meg has had a huge crush on her hot older boss for some time now. Could it be possible that her crush is reciprocated? https://BookHip.com/MNVVPBP

ALSO BY EMILY HAYES

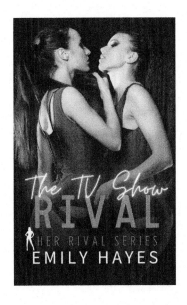

If you liked this one, I think you will love the next book
in the Her Rival Series! mybook.to/HR3